THIS ONE'S GOING TO LAST FOREVER

Also by Nairne Holtz

The Skin Beneath

THIS ONE'S GOING TO LAST FOREVER

NAIRNE HOLTZ

INSOMNIAC PRESS

The following stories have previously been published in slightly different
form: "When Gay is the New Straight," in *Velvet Mafia;* "No Parking," in
Lust for Life: Tales of Sex and Love (Vehicule, 2006); "Just the Man to
Straighten Her Out," in *Other Voices;* and "Phantoms," in
Blithe House Quarterly.

Library and Archives Canada Cataloguing in Publication
Holtz, Nairne, 1967-
This one's going to last forever / Nairne Holtz.

ISBN 978-1-897178-80-5

I. Title.

PS8615.O455T48 2009   C813'.6   C2009-901098-4

The publisher gratefully acknowledges the support of the Canada Council, the Ontario Arts Council, and the Department of Canadian Heritage
through the Book Publishing Industry Development Program.

Printed and bound in Canada

Insomniac Press
520 Princess Avenue
London, Ontario, Canada, N6B 2B8
www.insomniacpress.com

Canada Council   Conseil des Arts
for the Arts   du Canada   ONTARIO ARTS COUNCIL
                                    CONSEIL DES ARTS DE L'ONTARIO

Canada

For friends and lovers

"In the end one loves one's desire and
not what is desired."
—Friedrich Nietzsche, *Beyond Good and Evil*

TABLE OF CONTENTS

PART ONE

WHEN GAY IS THE NEW STRAIGHT

"Quick, I've got to write a poem. Give me your pen."
Nancy springs out of the front seat of her car. She yanks a
black marker from my hand, nearly breaking my fingers.
Not that she notices. She's interrupting her own wedding
vows to scribble on an empty coffee container, overcome
by her need to compose. She doesn't look like the bohemian
type. She's dressed in khakis and Gore-Tex, a regulation
Chap Stick dyke if I've ever seen one, but of course, clothes
don't *always* make the person.

I should know. I'm dressed in a white, flared polyester
jumpsuit with a chunky belt, Elvis in his Las Vegas period.
My outfit is a perfect facsimile of Elvis's Chinese Dragon
suit, covered in intricate beading designs that I sewed myself. A white scarf ensnares my neck and a gold medallion
nuzzles my chest. Unlike Elvis, I keep my chest shaved.
There are limits to what I will do for this job. In a former
life, I lived in Toronto, where I partied too much and
worked as a corporate temp. Now I live in Sudbury, a city
that resembles the cratered surface of the moon, a wasteland in which vegetation has been decimated by logging and
acid rain. I impersonate the King for my job, performing

weddings for my Uncle Joe's drive-through wedding chapel specializing in elopements. At $99.99, his wedding ceremony is cheaper than going to city hall.

I have a slight resemblance to Elvis. I have his dark, expressive eyebrows, a fullness to my lips and softness to my cheeks, sparkles of femininity that in my twinky days made me a man magnet, but have turned to puffiness now that I'm on the wrong side of thirty. My Uncle Joe, in his heyday, was a better impersonator. Now he's too old to be Elvis, even in his bloated, coke-addled days.

Sylvie, the "groom," a short French-Canadian woman who has selected black jeans and a long-sleeved white shirt for her big day, gets out of the car to inspect the plastic garlands of flowers surrounding my booth, the Crystal Wedding Chapel. Two kids remain strapped in the back seat, faces and hands twitching as if they have Tourette's, calling to Nancy, clearly their biological mother, no doubt from an earlier heterosexual union: "Mom, I want to go to Burger King! Mom, he stole my toy! Mom, do you have to write a poem?" The kids are delegates at an attention deficit disorder conference.

I glance at my watch. I have another couple booked in a quarter of an hour. Fridays are always busy. I hope Nancy is writing a haiku. Her need to write reminds me of the men (and they always seem to be men) who aim video cameras with the intensity of a sniper, taping weddings and the kids' birthday parties I also do. When recording your experience is more important than having your experience, something is wrong. I'm not sure why, but this videotaping feels like gathering evidence for a future cover-up.

Nancy waves her poem in the air and announces she'll read it before she and Sylvie put on their rings. I suggest that the two of them might want to get back into their car first. My tone must have been off, because Sylvie whips her head around at me like a terrier catching the sound of an intruder. Nonetheless, they get into the car, Sylvie opting for the driver's seat. Nancy puts one hand on her chest and reads her poem in a singsong voice: "You give me love that burns / A sunbather hopping across hot sand / Your hand enters / canyons of my desire / Our journey of love transcends time and place." Sylvie watches her with the smitten benevolence of someone who is whipped as hell.

"I pronounce you partners in life," I say. They are my first same-sex couple, now that marriage is legal for gays in this province. I redrafted the standard vows with care, made sure every sentence was inclusive. When gay marriage first became legal, I was actually quite sincere in looking forward to marrying gay men and lesbians. I thought it might be an opportunity for me to be more sincere generally, as if all that was wrong was not the ceremony itself, but my exclusion from the process. I wanted to stop watching the groom, thinking, Yum—what a waste: I wanted to stop trashing the bridesmaids' dresses in my head, and making them over with my own, much improved designs. Yes, even though this is a drive-through, there are still often bridesmaids. I thought I might be moved for a change, but it doesn't happen. As I watch Nancy slip a silver band over Sylvie's finger, I think, Just Assimilated. What will happen to desire when gay becomes the new straight? Am I being bitchy, or is it just that my first gay customers are such a tiresome cliché?

In the afternoon, I get a call from a babbling woman. She wants to book a wedding. The problem is, she twitters, she isn't sure her boyfriend will agree to marry her. She plans to propose this weekend.

Honey, if you gotta pop the question, it ain't gonna

happen, I think.

"He's always said his family is the reason he doesn't want to get married. Because they're Finnish, they'll insist on a huge, expensive wedding with relatives coming over from Finland, and we'll have to eat rye bread and herring. So I thought . . ." She pauses for a breathy titter. "What if we just elope? I mean, his family can't be mad at him forever. Especially if we have a baby. I mean, my boyfriend really wants kids."

I reach for the appointment book. "If you want a quick and dirty wedding, this is the place."

She giggles again. "Well, I hope it's not dirty. My boyfriend is Mr. Clean. His apartment is spotless. And you know, before I started seeing him, I never bothered ironing my clothes. But he irons everything. His jeans. His T-shirts. Even his underwear. And he folds them. Now I iron everything. It takes a lot of work, but it does feel nice against your skin. Do you know what I mean?"

I close my appointment book. "The chapel is perfectly clean. But this is a drive-through. You don't get out of your car. The ceremony takes only five minutes."

"That's okay, so does he." She pauses. "Was that too much information?"

Before I can stop myself, I chime in, "Not at all. My boyfriend's a preemie too."

Silence. I guess I went too far. Coming out as a queer is a bad idea in the blue-collar land of fag bashers and fundies.

Then she says, "Is he also Finnish?"

There are a fair number of Finns in this part of Ontario. "Uh, yeah, he is." The horrifying possibility that we might have the same boyfriend wavers in front of me, but I dismiss it.

She continues, "My boyfriend's a big fan of Elvis. That's why I thought of you. We met you when you performed at his twin nephews' birthday party."

I hold the receiver a little away from me, staring at it as if it's a nuclear device about to detonate. I remember the twin boys from that party two years earlier when I couldn't keep my eyes off Otto, a short man with an ass worthy of a ballet dancer. He had shaken his blond hair from his eyes to look at me, and then looked away when I checked him out. But I knew that we sang in the same choir. What I can't remember is his girlfriend. Tracy—that's her name—left no impression, was totally beige. But I know Otto will marry her.

After work, I meet Otto at a motel just outside town. This is what we do on Fridays during the horizon of afternoon and evening, our illicit but predictable cocktail hour. Otto likes to watch porn on cable television while I play with his tits. He pretends to be bored and indifferent while I pinch his nipples to pinpricks, lower my mouth over his dick and suck it until he moans.

Today I suggest we talk, which baffles him. Otto switches tactics, gets aggressive. While I remove my watch, he grabs me and orders me to bend over. When I protest (while wiggling my ass against his hard-on), he pushes me into the green chenille bedspread. He unhooks my belt and peels my pantsuit down. He likes me to wear my work clothes. He steps away, smacks my ass with the belt. Not having my attention makes him mean, and he starts talking to me in a way that would normally make him cringe. I get so hard that I don't even need to touch myself when he slips his wrapped cock into me. He comes fast, as usual. But he surprises me by being ready for another round after I come. He slides both his hands over my nipples, flips me over, and jerks himself off on my stomach. I lie back with my limbs gripping the bed, a quiet starfish, not chattering to him about my clients as I usually do.

"Is something wrong?" he asks. He hazards a guess. "Has your father gotten worse?"

My father has Alzheimer's. I moved up north to help my Uncle Joe look after him. My mother died ten years ago in a car accident, so it was my Uncle Joe who first noticed something was wrong with Dad. Joe came home to a flooded house after my father fixed a faucet leak for him. My father was a handyman who could repair anything. He had made his living as an electrician.

I tell Otto that no, things are better with my father because he forgets that he forgets.

Otto nods. "Like retarded kids who don't know they're stupid."

Otto is so up north. He doesn't know better than to say "retarded" or "Indian." Yet he doesn't hate people who aren't like him. A bit of hostility towards the Swedish for historical reasons, but that's about it.

"I married two dykes today," I say.

Otto stares at me. "You can do that now?"

"Don't you read the papers?" I ask, knowing he doesn't. I don't even know why I'm being so catty. I'm not in love with him. I don't want to marry him and persuade a member of the opposing team to inseminate for cash, or adopt a litter of Children's Aid kids with fetal alcohol syndrome. What bothers me is that the question of taking our relationship to another level never comes up, even after two years of clandestine meetings in motels and one weekend in a city four hours away where we went bowling together and shared chicken wings in a family restaurant. I've never had sex with anyone for a longer stretch than with Otto. Shouldn't passion count for something?

I continue, "I thought I'd be happy for them, but I didn't give a fuck." In the whole time I've been working at the chapel, only one couple touched my heart: a hunky Italian boy barely out of his teens marrying an older Aboriginal woman who made her living singing country western in the bars. Their desire was like a comet tearing a hole in the sky.

Otto isn't listening. He's looking out the window across the parking lot at the rocks, cracked and bleeding silt, dirt, and water. The city we live in was formed by a meteorite that seared a crater in the earth over a billion years ago. The debris and fallout material surrounding the crater became a rich mineral deposit. If I smash everything, will I be left with a gem?

"I think we should end this relationship," I say. Elvis has left the building.

On weekends, I look after my father because the live-in nurse gets two days off. I shower and dress my dad, brush his teeth, both his real ones and his partial dentures. I change his adult diapers. I show him where the cereal bowls are just as I did the day before because he can't remember. His brain shoots blanks; cell by cell, he's dying.

When my father was first diagnosed, he denied the disease. Then he got depressed, which he also refused to acknowledge: "Just lost some weight. Why you asking?" For me, his sequence of emotional responses was all too familiar because it was how he had dealt with my being a fag. When I was a teenager, he made me fix cars with him. I sulked and screwed the wrong parts together in acts of sabotage he pretended not to notice. His anger erupted when he and Mom visited me in Toronto and met my nelly roommate, who really was just a roommate. My father left my house before he could unpack, while an emotional self-discipline I never wanted swallowed my words, my hurt, because boys don't shriek, they rage, because boys don't cry when they lose. The aftermath? A crater where there had been a family of sorts, absence where there should have been presence.

These days, I have to remind him he is my father, and sometimes I just don't want to.

After I dump Otto, I drop by the mall to pick up a book for my dad on car racing. For some reason, my father can remember being a kid, and he's developed a fondness for what thrilled him then: fast cars.

At The Shirt Shack, I buy him a T-shirt that says, "Been There. Done That. Can't Remember." A T-shirt made for good old boys who have had a few too many. The vendor doesn't realize he has a niche market in seniors suffering from dementia. When I give my father the shirt, he chuckles. That's my cue; I laugh too. But then he cries, and I feel terrible.

"I'm afraid," he says.

I look at him, a scarecrow in his brown cardigan. He's slipping towards seventy-five, and his hooked nose looks like it's going to jump off the loose skin on his face. His hair is white tinged with yellow streaks, dog piss in the snow. We share the same build and features; I'm looking at my future. I pat his back, offer him a smoke. He puts his hand up like the sun is in his eyes. Recently, he's lost the desire to smoke. It's as if his adulthood and adolescence have melted away leaving me with an ancient child. It's the closest I will come to being a parent. It's the closest I will come to having a domestic partner. Maybe it's the closest I want to be. It's not like legalizing gay marriage has made me want to go get married. It's probably a lot like legalizing pot: whether it's legal or not, you either smoke it or you don't.

On Monday, a woman turns up as I'm closing the chapel. I'm clad in my usual attire, ersatz Elvis, his King of Spades suit this time. The woman is wearing mismatched business casual from Goodwill and has dyed purple hair spun out like cotton candy. She looks like Cyndi Lauper's small-town sister who never left home. What's weird about her is that despite the getup, she isn't a teenager. No, she's closer to thirty, the unpopular office secretary that everyone wants to vote off the island and won't sit next to on United Way Pizza Luncheon Day.

The woman sticks her hand out. "I'm Tracy. We spoke last week. I just wanted to see you."

Before I can shake her hand, she starts crying, her liquid eyeliner striping her freckled cheeks.

"He doesn't want to get married," I guess. Otto's girl-friend. Heartbreak Hotel.

"I asked him if there was someone else. He said there used to be, and that's why he couldn't marry me. He said he could manage being bi. He could be my husband if he had a boyfriend, but he doesn't anymore."

"Tracy," I begin.

Tracy wags her finger at me. "No, I don't need to know the details. It wasn't too hard to figure out. There aren't very many gays in this town."

"You'd be surprised," I say. I hand her a Kleenex from a package in my pocket.

She wipes her smeared makeup, tilts her chin at me.

"You know, I didn't want kids anyways. My sister's kids are such brats. I don't know how she stands them. If I'm at the mall with them for more than ten minutes, I fantasize about wacky Christians snatching them, kidnappers who wouldn't interfere with them but who might teach them not to expect so damn much."

I want to thank her for feeling the way she does, but instead I offer her a banality about not everyone being cut out for parenthood. It turns out a little goes a long way.

She sniffs. "My sister and parents feel sorry for me. They're always telling me not to worry, that I'll settle down and have kids, too. I want to tell them that's what I'm afraid of."

"Tracy, would you like to go out for a drink with me?" Tracy doesn't realize it, but she needs to come out, too. She's a born fag hag, strange and dramatic. I can't help it, I like her.

Tracy's eyes go slitty for a moment, carrying the suspicion people up here always have towards the unexpected. But even up here, some people realize the unexpected can be a gift, a geode in which sliced granite reveals the sheen of a gem. Tracy relaxes, gives me a tiny smile. "You're on," she says.

NO PARKING

She was driving one of those discreetly expensive cars—you could mistake it for a Volvo if you didn't know better, but I knew cars. She got out of her Renault and gave my co-worker Steve a hug. I wondered how a babe like her knew a loser like him. He was a pasty-faced guy whose jeans and T-shirts were always on the crusty side, as if every morning he spilled cereal on them. He'd finished high school eight years earlier and been working at the garage ever since—for a buck over minimum wage. He thought he was going to make it in the music biz. Please.

She was a classic beauty: Catherine Deneuve in *The Hunger*. Her face was fleshier and heavier at the jaw than Deneuve's, but I liked that. She seemed sensuous; I could imagine her slurping down oysters and kissing me greedily. She was pretty-in-punk: tall and curvy, long blonde hair with black streaks, wearing a black minidress with ripped black tights and scuffed army boots. I also wore army boots but never dresses. When she disappeared into the lower depths of the parking garage, I scooted out of my booth and over to Steve.

"Who's that chick you were talking to? She looks really

familiar," I lied. Steve knew I was gay, but I didn't want him to tell his friend, who was probably straight, that a dyke he worked with had the hots for her.

"Nathalie? She used to hang out with my brother. She wants to take pictures of my band for some kind of project." Steve winked at me. "Sexy, eh?"

I hadn't fooled him. "Think she'd want to take pictures for my zine?" I put out an independent magazine called *Girls with Guitars*. "Could you introduce us before she leaves?"

"No problem, dude." Being called "dude" gave me a thrill and notched up my respect for him.

Steve stretched his neck farther out of his booth to speak to me in a lower tone. "She likes chicks."

"She does?" My heart jammed like I had taken speed.

Nathalie drove through my booth an hour later while Steve was arguing with a customer, so I introduced myself to her and babbled about my zine. She listened attentively, making no attempt to rush off. I gave her my phone number when I noticed the cars in my line trying to pull over to Steve's booth. She handed me a ticket for a show she was going to the next night.

"Thanks." I shoved the ticket into my pocket. "If I'm not working, I'll check it out."

I acted really cool, but I could not believe my luck. It was like getting a date with the prom queen, except she had more of an edge: more high-school slut than cheerleader. She had to know I was a dyke. Since I had shaved my head and started dressing in black Levis and plaid shirts with the sleeves cut off, straight people assumed I was a man, fags hit on me like I was a twink until their eyes hit my crotch, but queer women recognized me as one of their own.

The next night, I turned up at the club, a place with

dark walls, no windows, and a black shag carpet on the floor strewn with ashes and cigarette butts. It was like walking on a giant expanse of pubic hair infested with crabs. The band playing on the riser at the back was a metal-funk group with four white guys. The bass player was getting a good freak on, and I watched his hands as they slapped and tickled his instrument. He both worshipped and possessed it. I wished I could jam like him, make my hands fly without thinking about what I was doing.

I arrived late—I hate waiting for girls. As I had hoped, Nathalie was already there. She looked super-cool. She had on the same torn tights and army boots as the day before, but instead of a minidress she wore a tank top and tiny black cut-offs with *FUCK* sloppily sewn on the back left pocket and *OFF* on the back right. I smiled when I read the message. I drank a couple bottles of beer and checked out her sexy ass, which was pouty yet firm. She ran around and talked to various guys, a big camera swinging from her neck. She took some pictures of the band, and finally, she came over to me. She kissed me hello on both cheeks.

She slid into the back booth I had scoped out, sat very close to me, and put her camera on the table. She stared at the band while I peeled the label off my beer bottle. When the set ended, she asked me what kind of pictures I needed for my zine.

The truth was I did not need a photographer. I had one, Liz, an artist who also did collages of mutants, little girls, and Siamese twins that cracked the edge of cute. But I had to tell Nathalie something, so I suggested she take pictures of all-girl bands.

"All-girl bands?" Nathalie sneered. "Like who? There's Dairy Queen, but Cat, their lead singer, fucking hates my guts. You know what she said to me once? She said,

'Nathalie, you take pictures of boys because you don't know how to be in the picture.' All because I once slept with a guy she was in love with."

Cat's voice sounded like a distraught chipmunk's, but the Dairy Queen girls were great eye candy. Too bad Nathalie wasn't on better terms with them.

Nathalie leaned over so her face was closer to mine. Her grey eyes were flecked with light—polished spoons. She sniffed. "You know, you smell like tea."

Tea? That was so crunchy. I wanted to smell like sin. "It's sandalwood."

"Maybe I'm getting confused between some tea and some incense I bought at the health food store."

I felt relieved, then awkward. I had managed to remove my beer label intact, and I folded it into a square. I hated the beginning part of getting to know someone. But I rarely got past that way-too-familiar experience. I'd had a few flings since I'd come out, but only one steady lover, and she had split her time between me and a guy, then dumped both of us for a woman that even I mistook for a man.

"Hi, Nathalie." A tall, thin boy wearing a long black leather coat stood in front of us holding a pitcher of beer in one hand and two glasses in the other. Goth Boy stared intently at Nathalie with his eyeliner-rimmed eyes.

"*Salut*, Paul." Nathalie avoided his gaze, but she bumped her hip against mine to move over and make room for him. After I slid over, she sat with her hip pressed against mine and opened her palm in my direction. "This is Nicky, the woman with the zine I was telling you about."

"What's it called?" Paul put a bony hand on her arm, but she shrugged it away. We were all skinny and hardly took up half the large, dark vinyl booth, and yet I felt like I had no room. We were three burning matches in a box.

— 26 —

"*Girls with Guitars*," I said.

"Never heard of it." Paul tucked his long hair behind an ear. "And I'm in a band, so I read music zines."

"It's a queer riot-grrrl zine, so I'm not surprised." I wanted to get the lesbian thing out in the open and make him realize he wasn't the only one who had a potential claim on Nathalie. If Nathalie had been with a guy, Paul never would have sat down without asking.

"Riot grrrl, eh? I support the movement. Too bad most of the bands suck," Paul said.

"Yeah, like most punk bands are so great," I retorted.

"What bands are you talking about? I don't think I've heard a riot grrrl band," Nathalie said while she poured a beer for him in one of the glasses he had brought over and a second one, which she set between us.

"I guess you're not into feminism." Paul gave us both a fat smirk.

"I've been away for two years," Nathalie snapped.

"Oh yeah. With André." Paul looked away from her and drank his beer.

The band started again, and I was happy to have an excuse not to talk to him. Maybe Nathalie was, too. I put my hand on her thigh and began tracing the seams of her shorts with my fingers. I wanted her ass across my lap and her shorts pulled down. The slogan on the back pockets of her shorts was far from original, but it was effective. She was the haughty girl that guys liked to claim "provoked" them—an attitude I thought was beneath me but felt anyway. I curled my fingers into a fist, jamming them between Nathalie's legs while she bit her lip. When she slunk down to allow me to touch more of her, I rolled my knuckles back and forth and snuck a look at Paul. I didn't think he knew what was going on, but I didn't care if he did. Getting to

— 27 —

do what I wanted turned me on.

When he got up to get more beer, Nathalie purred, "It's sexy when you sneak around."

I pulled my hand away. "Is he your boyfriend?"

"No. My lover. *Was* my lover. I dumped him last night."

I hadn't expected that. Emotions I might have felt towards her puckered like skin in the cold. Did she expect us to fight over her? I said nothing, but my face must have because when she started talking again, her tone was defensive.

"He saw me in the lineup of a club and decided I was the girl for him. He's an idiot. He doesn't know me, but he thinks he's in love with me. I told him I had a boyfriend, but that didn't matter to him. So we had a fling."

She had a boyfriend. Her parking lot was full. Did I leave or drive around? In my experience, it's always best to drive around. A space could open up, be yours if you grabbed it before the other guy circling around did.

"André and I are breaking up, but we still live together. I don't have the money right now to get my own place."

At the end of the evening, I shared a cab with Nathalie. She complained a lot about André, but she went home to him.

A few days later, Nathalie drove her Renault into my parking garage. I didn't notice her until she knocked on the glass door of my booth. I let her in. Seeing Nathalie in the daytime felt strange. The booze and dark club had made conversation easy and intimate. But she acted as if we were old pals. She sat on the only seat, a stool, and talked to me about travelling in Asia, where she and André had taught English in Korea and Japan, then used their savings to hang out in

Thailand and Bali. She missed travelling; it took her out of herself and made the club scene seem irrelevant. She read a lot of books while travelling, stuff on Zen Buddhism, the history of Cambodia and Japan, art. Reading kept her from having to deal with her boyfriend.

"Why'd you go to Asia with him?" I asked.

"To get away from my boyfriend before him." Nathalie fidgeted with some woven Guatemalan bracelets on her slender arm. "I was in a relationship with this guy who wouldn't let go. He was stalking me, and I had to get a restraining order against him."

Men, men, men. "Have you ever had a relationship with a woman?" I asked.

"I dated this girl when I was nineteen, but she was a troublemaker. She was really macho. It was okay for a while, but I used to be afraid she would get too drunk one night, call my family, and tell them I was a lesbian."

For some reason, I remembered the first time I had kissed a girl back in ninth grade at a sleepover party. Truth, dare, double-dare, promise-to-repeat. *Dare.* I dare you to kiss me. I'd poked my tongue through lips that tasted like Dubble Bubble gum and that drew away from mine. *Ew, why'd you french me?* I'd protested that it was a game, but fear had lobbed around my brain.

"Do you get a lunch break?" Nathalie was looking me straight in the eye.

Steve covered for me for half an hour while I followed Nathalie down a level to her car. She got into the driver's seat, reached over, and opened the passenger door for me to get in.

"There's some pot in the glove compartment," she said.

I clicked open the lid, and car registration papers fell onto my lap. I picked them up and put them back in the glove compartment, noticing as I did that André was the owner of the Renault. I found a small baggie of pot and handed it to Nathalie. She rolled us a joint and lit it using the dashboard lighter. As she handed me the spliff, she said, "You know, it's refreshing to have someone not feel sorry for me when I told them I was stalked."

I nodded before inhaling. I, too, hated having people feel sorry for me although it didn't happen often.

I pinched the joint after we had smoked about half of it. The weed was good quality, and I didn't want to get too wasted since I had to work. Nathalie, sprawled next to me in a stupid torpor, didn't protest. My eyes fuzzily followed her collarbone down to an edge of black lace cupping her breasts. Her beauty was intimidating, but I was a woman who took dares, so I put my arms around her and kissed her. She didn't put her tongue in my mouth, but she kept her mouth open and wound her hands around my neck. After a while, she pushed me against the seat. She was very quiet, which made me nervous. Was she enjoying herself?

She pulled my T-shirt up over my braless breasts, exposing them.

"God, I could kill you—you have the breasts of a teenage girl." Nathalie leaned back into the driver's seat, surveying me.

You're supposed to want my breasts, not want to have them, I thought.

"Whenever I have sex with André, I feel like he should have breasts," Nathalie said.

An unwelcome image of Nathalie running her hands through the chest hair of a naked guy rolled through my mind. I distracted myself by reaching behind her and un-zipping her black cotton dress. I leisurely brushed each of her shoulder straps down and unhooked her bra. She had the kind of body some women get surgery for. Her nipples were large and pale as sand dollars, and I leaned over and took one of them into my mouth, sucking it into a pink tip. Then I kissed the other breast. Nathalie's breath sharpened, and she moved her head from side to side. But then she drew away and zipped her dress back up. She leaned over, cupped my face in her hands, and kissed me so softly that I knew it was over—whatever it was.

I went on a bunch of dates with Nathalie over the next month, but we didn't have sex. We went drinking at straight bars where Nathalie knew a lot of boys-in-bands who talked to her about "making it, really making it, not just in Quebec or Canada, but in L.A., man." I tolerated this, barely. I had to worry more about strange boys flirting with her than about the man she lived with. She was such a shit to him: we'd be talking on the phone, and she'd put down the re-ceiver to yell at him for not buying the right brand of soy milk. I wasn't concerned about her running off with an-other woman: she had no female friends and was always putting down the girls in the music scene. I kept waiting for her to put me down, too.

As the weeks passed, I stopped being afraid she would run away. The problem was she stayed in place. When would we do more than make out? Did she not want me the way she wanted men? Her ambivalence kept my own desire in check.

One night we ran into my co-worker Steve and the rest of his band, the Dead Brain Cells. I had seen them play before but had never met the rest of them personally. Nathalie knew them and introduced me to everyone as "my friend Nicky." As she chatted with the guys, I stewed over the fact that she had pointedly called me her "friend." We were more than that. Tonight I would pin her down on what exactly we were—after I had a few drinks.

The Dead Brain Cells didn't talk to Nathalie for long; they were on their way to a gig. As they walked away, both Nathalie and I overheard one of them say to Steve, "How do you know that fag she's with?"

Another guy chimed in: "Is there something you're not telling us?"

"Nicky's a girl I work with, not a guy." Steve increased his pace.

"*Tabarnac!*"

Nathalie gave me an apologetic look.

I shrugged. They were dickheads, but I was used to that sort of thing: homophobic ripples in my day. I didn't usually get hassled when I was with Nathalie. Her beauty buffered me from the snarky comments of straight guys and the glares of straight chicks when I went to the bathroom in a het bar. I decided to take advantage of Nathalie feeling bad: "I want to go to a dyke bar tonight."

"Well, okay."

"What's the matter?"

"The music will suck." Nathalie wrinkled her nose.

She was right, but I wanted to be around my tribe. I also wanted to run into my ex-girlfriend. I hadn't spoken to my ex in months, even though she wanted us to be friends. I thought I might manage to speak to her with Nathalie pinned to me like a corsage. Nathalie was better looking than my ex.

Nathalie and I walked over to Huis Clos, a lesbian cocktail bar. The bar had originally been a first-floor apartment built in the early part of the twentieth century. Large stained glass windows were set into the building's greystone exterior. Inside, the bar was small—the regulation pool table barely fit into the back. You had to ask someone to move every time you took a shot. There was no dance floor, but the bartender had a boom box that played Dionne Warwick and Grace Jones.

"I like this place. I've never been here before." Nathalie arranged herself on a high bar stool.

I stood beside her, leaning across the bar to pay for our drinks. After I tipped the bartender, I scanned the room for my ex but instead caught the eye of my photographer, Liz. She was wearing a gingham dress, and her dark, crimped hair was pulled into two braided pigtails fastened by bright red baubles. She never dressed like a normal person; she always showed up everywhere in a costume. She cared more about art than about looking sexy. She came over to where I was standing and rested her scarred elbows on the edge of the bar.

"You know, Liz, you kind of look like Dorothy from *The Wizard of Oz*."

"Oh goodie," she said without sarcasm.

"Guess you're not in Kansas anymore." I tossed my head in the direction of all the women surrounding us. Neither Nathalie nor Liz smiled. "The Tin Man was my favourite character. What about you guys?"

"The Wicked Witch," Nathalie said. She sipped her Campari and lime through a straw. "I mean, Dorothy was pretty boring, always whining to go home. How pathetic is that? I'd like nothing better than to get the fuck out of here and travel to Asia again."

I leaned back and rested my elbows against the bar. Her

words stung; I was part of here.

Liz put her head in her hands, then looked up. "Toto. I liked Toto."

"By the way, I'm Nathalie." Nathalie extended her hand to Liz, who clasped it heartily.

"Sorry, I forgot my manners." I edged my tongue around my teeth—it felt as if something was caught, but I could find nothing. "Nathalie, this is Liz. She does art for my zine."

"Are you Nicky's girlfriend?" Liz ducked her head slightly.

"Kind of." Nathalie kept her tone light.

"I guess I'll see you guys around." Liz slid her elbows from the bar. I would not say she disappeared into the crowd—not in that outfit—but she moved away from us.

Nathalie poked my biceps with the straw from her drink. "You know, I usually can't tell when an anglophone wants to go to bed with someone, but that girl has a crush on you."

I shrugged. I knew Liz liked me, but I ignored it. Liz was so awkward. She couldn't make the patter a woman needed to survive and make friends in the dyke bars. She was a talented artist but too weird for me. I told Nathalie, "I'm not sure if she wants to have sex with me, but I think she might want to lie down naked together in a field and put body paint on me."

Nathalie snickered.

I took a sip of my beer. "What did you mean about not knowing when an English person wants to sleep with you?"

Nathalie laughed and an unexpected dimple appeared high on her cheek. "If you go to bed with a francophone, he will tell you, 'I like your toes. You have beautiful breasts. I love you. I love you.' He will be tender, whereas English guys often don't talk—it's a cliché, but they are more re-served in my experience. I can always tell when a French guy is flirting with me, but I'm never sure with an English guy."

I polished off the rest of my beer and set the bottle down with a clink. Was she trying to tell me something? I didn't tell her she was beautiful, but I often reassured her. Told her that her clothes looked great, that she was not hav-ing a bad hair day, that she didn't look fat. Didn't she un-derstand how I felt about her?

"When are you going to sleep with me?" I wanted to sound seductive, but a whine crept into my tone.

"Can't we just let it happen if it happens?"

"That's not good enough." Anger edged into my voice. "Either you want to or you don't." I glanced away from her, towards the women standing at the bar, and tried to find a cutie I could imagine doing, but it didn't work. I couldn't escape the humiliating situation I had put myself in as I waited for her to say something.

"All right. Let's go to your place now. I can't spend the night, though." Nathalie refused to look at me, just gulped down the rest of her drink. We left the bar and hailed a cab from the street. She got into the front of the cab, leaving me to get into the back by myself even though I was the one who directed the cab driver. I felt like I was bringing a prostitute home. Not that I ever had, but that was what popped into my head.

When we got to my apartment, Nathalie surveyed my living room and made the joke everyone did about how it looked like I had just moved in. Most of my furniture and utensils were stuff you used when you went camping. I had visited her place last week when André was at work. Their apartment had a definite look—something that had clearly required a lot of effort. The rooms were painted yellow and burgundy and olive with many carved mahogany boxes and chests that I later found out were Balinese. There were glass jars filled with marbles, leafy plants on antique oak plant stands, and pillows covered in Thai silk. If Nathalie was planning to move out of that apartment, she was not leaving soon.

I went into the kitchen to fix us some drinks and was surprised, when I came out, to find her lying in my bed, under the covers but clearly naked. I would have preferred to undress her myself, but I didn't say anything. I set our drinks on the floor, got under the covers with her, and nibbled her neck, which was acrid with smoke. She slipped her hands under my T-shirt and began to pull it over my head. I let her take my shirt off, exposing my breasts, but when she started undoing my belt buckle, I stopped her. She was moving too fast, and I wasn't ready. I wasn't sure I could be ready. I was scared to let her do something to me and then notice that she found it gross. She never talked about women, about wanting them. It was always men, men, men.

"I want to fuck you," I told her, hoping that saying it would make me want to. I had never been so nervous with a woman. I put my thumb under her chin and tilted her head back. I remembered her saying she liked bad boys in bed, nasty motherfuckers, as she disconcertingly called them, so I tried to be that bad boy. I sucked her nipples, pulled her hair, and then spread her open and sucked her clit. The noises she made were slight, barely encouraging, so I stopped. She had left a streak of wetness on my chin, however, so I began to fuck her with my hand. When she groaned, I felt relieved. I tucked all my fingers and thumb into her and wished I had an expensive latex dildo. I wondered if she would like it or find it stupid and fake compared with a guy. After a few minutes, she pushed her cunt over my knuckles and squirmed in a quick orgasm. My own response was more cerebral: pride at making her come rather than being turned on myself.

She lay still, and then rolled over and asked if there was anything she could do for me. I shook my head because I could not get over the feeling that she would just be doing me as a favour. I had thought that making her come would make everything right, affirm that, yes, she wanted to be doing this, that she wanted to be with me, but her coming cracked apart whatever there was between us.

"I should go. André . . ." Nathalie let the sentence trail off as she yanked her dress and panties back on and laced up her army boots. She put her bra in the pocket of her leather jacket.

"I'll walk you to the metro."

As we walked to the subway, Nathalie chattered about how impossible it was to go shopping with her mother, who bought her clothes that were ugly and too large and who complained about her daughter's weight. "She wants me to be fat like her," Nathalie said with disgust.

I felt annoyed, distant. Why did she care if someone else was fat? The gap between us reminded me of seventh grade when all the girls in my class stopped playing games, training-bra mania began, and I just didn't get it.

When we got to the stairs leading down to the metro, I leaned over to kiss her, but she pulled away.

"Don't. Someone . . . one of André's friends could see us."

After that, I didn't call her and she didn't call me. Two weeks had passed when Steve came up to me while I was on break,

— 37 —

reading next to the Coke machine.

"So you're not seeing Nathalie anymore," he said.

"Yeah, well, she's straight. That's the last time I go out with a straight chick." I continued to look at my book as if I were reading, but I couldn't concentrate. Was Nathalie a lesbian? I just knew how equivocal her desire for me had felt. Nathalie competed with other women and was scared shitless to be a dyke, but that didn't mean she wasn't one.

Steve's Coke clanged to the bottom of the machine, but he ignored it. "That's not what I heard. She said you acted aggressive, like a guy"—here he waggled his eyebrows so I'd know that he knew she meant *in bed*—"and that was the last thing she wanted or expected from a woman."

"Bullshit!" I stood up, and my book fell to the ground. I was aghast that she had told him such intimate details. My hand squeezed into a fist, and I pounded the Coke machine.

"Hey, don't shoot the messenger." Steve bent over and pulled out his Coke. His jeans were too big around his skinny waist, and I could see half his butt.

"If I were a guy, we wouldn't be having this conversation." I picked up my book and stamped back to my booth. Thinking about her and her boyfriend that she pretended wasn't her boyfriend pissed me off. I remembered how her apartment had a vacuum cleaner and a stand-up freezer instead of just a broom and an icebox in the fridge. André was seven years older than she was and had a decent job. Nathalie liked his money, liked having a car. No way would I let her park that Renault in my garage again. If she tried, I would fold my arms across my chest and say, *"Excusez-moi, madame, mais vous ne pouvez pas stationner ici."*

I expected to run into Nathalie sooner or later, probably in a bar on St. Laurent, but less than a week after my conversation with Steve, I saw her downtown. I was on my bike, coming home from work. The streets were crammed and noisy. It was Grand Prix weekend, Montreal's Formula One racing event. There was a certain stupidity to having a car race in the middle of a smog alert, but nobody seemed to care. I stopped at a red light, then noticed Nathalie getting out of the passenger seat of the car beside me. The Renault was parked illegally. When the driver got out, Nathalie pointed to the sign at the corner. He squinted at it, gave her a naughty-boy grin, and then shrugged his shoulders.

"André!" Her frustration pierced the sluggish air. She drew glances from passersby, and not just for her looks.

Her boyfriend was blond and handsome, a fraternity brother in rumpled khaki shorts. I had expected him to be dull, proper, a suit with a humiliatingly large bald spot. Instead, he and Nathalie were attractive enough to appear on reality TV. Neither of them appeared to notice me.

"Nathalie," I called.

Her eyes met mine. She didn't move, but she looked like she wanted to steal off.

I dragged my bike over to the curb where she and André were standing. She had humiliated me at work; now it was her turn to suffer.

"What are you doing downtown?" I spoke to her with a rough intimacy, as if she were a teenager, and I were her father who had a right to know her business.

"André wants to see the new collection of Ferraris." She shifted her body so she was facing away from me.

André stuck out his hand. "Hi there. Don't think we've met. I'm André." His grip was professionally firm.

"Nice to meet you." I gave Nathalie an expectant stare.

"This is Nicky, a friend." Her tone was infused with a blandness that suggested she barely knew me. Francophones were expert at using politeness to convey disdain.

My heart hopscotched. "Yeah, right. Friends call each other when they have something to say. And friends don't fuck."

Nathalie gasped, but it was André's reaction that I watched: his silky smile fading; the pinch of his eyes as he appraised me before concluding my threat level was green—low risk. Still, measures were required. He grabbed Nathalie's arm. "Payback for Namiko?"

She slammed her elbow backwards, ripping her arm from his grasp. "Not everything's about you, you know." She scowled at both of us now.

André yanked his hand back, scowling at her in turn. He didn't say it, but the word "bitch" was all over his face.

Nathalie walked away, twisting quickly and purposefully through the crowd. André got back into his car and blasted his horn to pry a space through the people scrambling around, the long honks signalling his anger. I stood on the sidewalk, ignoring the hostile stares of pedestrians annoyed that my bike was blocking their way.

Just the Man to Straighten Her Out

Valerie checked the time on the corner of her computer screen. Ten minutes until lunch. She emailed Ian, one of her co-workers at the medical supply company, and asked if he wanted to grab a bite to eat. Valerie was a "knowledge officer," which basically meant getting stuff for people, while Ian managed the local area network. They had started talking about a month ago after he admired her trolls. Other women in the office put up pictures of their babies and husbands, while she kept a collection of trolls on her desk. Some of the trolls were beautifully designed Scandinavian kids' toys made from wood and fur and cloth while others, acquired at yard sales, were plastic figurines with fluorescent hair.

Ian was Valerie's first straight male friend. With her chubby figure, pale, round face, and cloud of dark, frizzy hair, she was the sort of woman gay men felt comfortable around and straight men didn't notice. This was fine with Valerie, since she was a lesbian. A fag friend at work would have been cool, but as far as she could tell, no one was gay.

Finding gay friends outside work was also a problem.

The only person Valerie hung out with in Toronto was her straight-but-not-narrow sister, Becky. On the street and at queer events, Valerie saw plenty of cute dykes, but the lesbian community hadn't opened itself up to her the way it had in the university town she had left last year. In Guelph, being lesbians was enough of a basis to form relationships. Plus, Valerie had a girlfriend then, who had split up with her when she moved to Toronto. Why an hour's distance had prompted the demise of their relationship was a less interesting question than how they had sustained their relationship in the first place: Valerie's ex-girlfriend was an energetic jock who went to university mainly to play varsity basketball, while Valerie was an honours Anthropology student whose idea of a perfect weekend was to lie on the couch and read fantasy novels.

Click. A new email had arrived. It was from Ian, saying he was sorry, but he had already arranged to have lunch with Kim, his assistant. Valerie had observed that Kim had an anxious crush on Ian. Kim was a quiet twenty-year-old with glasses, long blonde hair, and a stunning body she made no effort to accentuate. She dressed in a bland style and didn't wear makeup. From Ian, Valerie knew that Kim, under parental duress, had been studying Business Administration. She hated it, so she was taking a break and working in her uncle's company. Valerie felt faintly superior to Kim, although she could not have said why exactly.

Valerie got up from her computer, retrieved the faux fur backpack that she used as a purse, and walked into the lunchroom. The company was located in an industrial wasteland far from downtown, so, without a car, it was impossible to escape the office during lunch hour. Valerie hated the lunchroom because she could never think of a single thing to say to the women, both secretaries and professionals, who congregated there. One time when they had talked about how much weight women gain on the pill, Valerie had chimed in about its health risks, prompting a woman to ask if Valerie was on the pill. Valerie had replied, "No, I'm a lesbian," and the woman had stared as though Valerie had three heads. Valerie didn't think it was a big deal to come out in this day and age, but her comment had squeezed all the conversation from the room.

As Valerie took her frozen vegetable quesadilla out of the freezer and stuck it into the microwave, she heard the women talking about their kids. One woman said, "Tony's just like his daddy, likes to get his own way. Three years old, and he was all upset because he's not big enough to play hockey with his brothers. So what did he do? He stole their puck."

Another woman said, "He's all boy."

Valerie snorted as she took her lunch out of the microwave. Although she wasn't supposed to, she took her food back to her cubicle. At the end of her warren of cubicles, she spotted Ian and Kim dressed in their coats and walking towards the elevator. Valerie felt . . . jealous. Ian was tall and boyish with ginger hair. He stooped when he walked, and he had delicate freckles covering his nose, cheeks, and eyelids that Valerie rather liked. She had never had sex with a man before, but she was attracted to him. Behind her, she heard her trolls mutter, "These cross-cultural things never work out."

A few days later, Valerie went to see her sister Becky to talk about her crush on Ian. She didn't know whether Ian was attracted to her, but her sense of men was that they were often ready for something casual. Besides, if he wasn't interested, what did she have to lose?

Becky worked evenings, so Valerie dropped in on her sister at the office. Her sister had found a job as a phone-sex worker through her long-standing boyfriend, William, a hippie who was a telephone psychic and astrologer. Becky had been tired of her job as a bike courier and started phone sex as a lark, but the money had kept her there for almost two years. She was good at it. She had received an award for the longest hold time.

Fantasy Island Phones was located in a generic office building in a strip mall. Inside the building, everything was a shade of blue or cream. The carpets and curtains were ecru, the melamine desks were indigo, and the walls were a dazzling cerulean. Valerie kept expecting Mr. Roarke to materialize from behind a cubicle toasting everyone with a glass of champagne. Becky had explained that the colours were supposed to create a sense of tranquility. Despite the seediness of the work, Fantasy Island Phones had a rather benevolent environment. On the night Valerie turned up, all the women were in pyjamas for "casual night" and the supervisors had ordered pizza.

Valerie found her sister talking on the phone with her long legs sprawled across the desk. Becky was wearing baggy skater pants and a stained L7 T-shirt. Her sister had not gone casual because her usual nightwear was a pair of boxer shorts and a T-shirt. When Valerie had told her parents she was a lesbian, they had been perplexed. "We thought Becky might turn out to be lesbian," they had said. This was because Becky was a tomboy, whereas the one part of being a typical girl Valerie had resisted was the part about liking boys. Until recently, anyway.

When Becky looked up, she put a finger to her lips. "I'm a voluptuous lass with a pale plump bottom," she said in a passable Scottish accent. She had warned Valerie that she had been attempting to enliven the work by using different accents.

"You're piercing my buttocks with that giant sword of yours." Becky began to moan. "Ay, that's a Highland claymore, that is."

Valerie giggled, and Becky held up a warning hand. Valerie moved out of the cubicle and waited for her to finish. A minute later, Becky motioned her sister back in. "What's up?"

There was no extra chair, so Valerie remained standing, her right hand clutching the fabric of her long skirt. "How do you have safe sex with a guy?"

Becky's face scrunched up with disbelief. "What?"

"Remember that guy I mentioned at my work, Ian? I'm kind of into him."

"Like, really into him?"

Valerie smoothed out the wrinkles she had created in her skirt and pondered the question. She didn't know Ian very well. They had good conversations in which they trashed their employer and discussed their favourite fantasy novels, but that "grrr" feeling she had had towards her exgirlfriend—at least in the beginning—was absent. She was more, well, bi-curious. "I wouldn't say I'm head over heels."

Becky stared at her thoughtfully. "Let's go for a break."

Valerie followed Becky through the cubicles. She had spent the last few days trying to talk herself out of having sex with Ian. She concentrated on the things about him that she found unattractive, like that he dressed badly. He wore acrylic sweaters that were too tight and jeans that were pulled up around his waist. But her mind would not co-operate; she continued to imagine having sex with him.

An older woman with hair dyed the colour of a sunset plucked Becky's sleeve. "I've got a joke for you."

"Yeah?" Becky gave the woman a skeptical smile but stopped to listen.

"Where's your asshole when you're having an orgasm?"

Becky shrugged.

"At home watching TV. Good one, eh?"

Becky laughed dryly.

"I don't get it," Valerie whispered after they had walked past the woman and into a boardroom where the employees took their coffee breaks.

"Asshole equals husband."

Valerie found this whole "men are from Mars, women are from Venus" mentality strange. It was so different from the feeling of tribal kinship she had towards other lesbians.

Becky took a seat and Valerie joined her. She listened as her sister gave her the breakdown on safe sex. It seemed to involve a tedious amount of preparation and lack of spontaneity. So much for those Hollywood movies that showed men abruptly pinning women to walls.

"That's a good thing about being pregnant," Becky said. She clapped her hand to her mouth. The words had just tumbled out.

"Oh my God." Valerie went over to Becky and hugged her. "That's why you haven't lit up a cigarette yet. You're pregnant." She looked down at her sister's belly, but her stomach didn't look any rounder than usual.

"I haven't taken the test yet, but I think so. William and I had sex without a condom, and three days later my breasts were like melons."

The following Monday, Valerie was taking a break and Googling herself only to discover that access to a website that mentioned her name was blocked. The site belonged to her university's gay and lesbian student group where she had been an active member. Installing a filtering program onto everyone's computer didn't seem like Ian's style, so she went to talk to him about it.

She found him in his office sitting in front of his computer, while Kim lurked over his shoulder.

Valerie said, "Did you install filters onto the server?"

Ian slowly spun his chair around, forcing Kim to step away from him. Ian looked up at Valerie with a pained expression. "The vice-president made me do it."

"Why? If they think someone is spending too much time on the Web, why don't they track how many hours they're surfing? Who gives a shit whether someone's checking movie listings or looking for a dominant woman?"

Ian sighed. "They did it because someone was going to porn sites and using them as screen savers on a bunch of computers."

Kim piped up. "The last time I borrowed a laptop, the whole screen was covered with breasts. God, I was so embarrassed!"

Valerie was reminded of something that had happened to her in high school. Some girls put a *Penthouse* centrefold in her locker after she had gotten drunk and made out with a girl from another school at a party. She remembered the absolute terror she had felt when she opened her locker and saw a picture of a naked woman with bad tan lines and a thin patch of brown pubic hair running down her crotch like a fuzzy caterpillar. She had ripped the picture down with a shaking hand, horrified at the idea of everyone thinking she was a dyke. Had Kim been embarrassed by the pornography for the same reason, or was that just something you felt when you actually were a lesbian?

Ian stood up and gestured towards his chair. "Valerie,

if you want, you can use my computer. It doesn't have a filter on it."

Valerie waved his offer away with her hand. "I don't need to see this particular site, which incidentally doesn't have any porn, but I'm concerned because filtering programs don't understand context, and someday I might need to look at a medical site that mentions enough body parts to get blocked."

Ian stammered, "L-l-like I said, it wasn't my idea."

A flush rose on Ian's cheeks, covering his adorable freckles, and Valerie felt the force field of invisible space that she and Ian maintained at work become liquid, permeable. Ian wanted her, Valerie, not Kim. Valerie had scooped him from Kim, which had its satisfactions. Kim reminded Valerie of every popular blond girl who had been hateful to her because she was a dyke and a nerd.

Back at her cubicle, the trolls were less impressed with Valerie's coup. "Competing for the male gaze. Have you already forgotten what you learned in your Women's Studies classes?"

Valerie glared at the trolls. "Don't judge me. You guys steal babies."

The trolls grinned fiendishly at her. "Yes, we're brutes, but we know it."

That was enough. Valerie turned the trolls around so that they faced the wall and weren't able to communicate with her. Then she opened her email and discovered that Ian had invited her for a drink after work.

She and Ian went to a nearby fern bar with booths and lots of woodwork. The crowd seemed to be other office workers. Over imported beer, Ian told Valerie that he hadn't been seeing anyone since splitting up with his last girlfriend.

Valerie thought he looked wistful when he said this. He

seemed like a man who liked the company of women, who felt lost without a girl. But everything he told her after his second beer was the sort of thing that would make any potential girlfriend run for the hills.

"I'm in counselling because I always get bored with my girlfriends after a few months and break up with them. I enjoy the hunt but not the catch, and I'm trying to understand why that is."

"Is that why you aren't dating Kim?" Valerie watched Ian carefully.

"I like Kim, but she's from a small town and she's never had sex before. She's kind of religious."

"I don't think she likes me very much."

"She's intimidated by you."

Valerie smiled and then sipped the last of her beer. She liked that. If she could not feel close to any of the women she worked with, it was fun to be the big bad wolf.

Ian raised his hand to motion to the waiter for another drink, but Valerie placed her hand on his arm. "Why don't we have a drink at my place?"

Ian paid the bill, insisting that it wasn't because he was sexist, but because he had asked her out. Then Ian drove Valerie to her apartment. He had a decent car, a navy blue Nissan. Valerie enjoyed not taking the subway. When they got to her place, Valerie realized that she had never gotten around to coming out to him.

She led Ian through her one-bedroom apartment, hoping he noticed the poster for a lesbian and gay film festival and the lesbian magazines. His gaze, however, had nervously settled on the fridge door, which had a picture of Hothead Paisan machine-gunning a group of men. They sat on her futon couch.

"Mostly I'm a lesbian," Valerie blurted out.

"Why me?" Ian's voice cracked like a teenager's.

Valerie shrugged. She was afraid to analyze her attraction to him because she wasn't sure that it would be flattering to either of them. She walked over to her CD player and put on Portishead. The spooky music seemed appropriate to her mood. It felt strange to be with a man in this way, but she had made the decision to go through with it, so she was calm.

When she sat down again, he kissed her. They necked on the couch for a long time, and Valerie enjoyed it. After a while, she lifted up his yellow sweater (a candidate for Goodwill) and played with his nipples. "Are your nipples sensitive?"

"I don't know. No one has touched them before."

Valerie had assumed nipple-sucking was a human instinct. Did most straight girls just lie back and let their boyfriends do them? God, this suddenly felt like an anthropological exercise. *The method I used to gather data on heterosexuality was participant observation.*

Ian undid the zipper on Valerie's long skirt and slipped his hand between her legs—that felt nice. It really had been a long time. But, when they began fucking, she was again distracted by comparisons. Ian's penis was much softer than a dildo or finger, and the sensations were so diffused. She was used to her ex-girlfriend's thin finger pressing with exquisite precision on her G-spot, but she suspected that asking a man to use his finger instead of his penis wouldn't go over well. But after they'd been fucking for a while with neither of them coming, she asked him to go down on her.

Ian said, "I'm not that into cunnilingus."

"Please tell me you're not squeamish." It was one of those bad clichés about straight men that Valerie had assumed couldn't be true.

"I prefer this." Ian pointed to his hard dick.

They fucked some more, but Valerie couldn't come, even when she touched herself. It was frustrating. What was really bizarre was that Ian couldn't come either. She would not let him thrust hard enough or something. In the end, he came by turning her over and using her thighs to masturbate with. Valerie wondered if he was gay.

"Have you ever been with a man?" Valerie demanded when the sex was over. She sat up with the sheet pulled tightly over her body. Another difference between Ian and her ex: her girlfriend would always tell Valerie her breasts were beautiful, her skin was soft.

Ian looked shocked. "No."

"Have you ever thought about it?"

"No. I like women." The volume of his voice crept up.

Valerie continued to interrogate him. "Is it different being with a woman who's attracted to women?" It felt strange to call herself a lesbian after what she had just done, but she wasn't ready to embrace the bisexual label.

"I find you fascinating." He rolled over on his side and patted her thigh. "I've written twenty pages about you in my journal."

Now Valerie was shocked. She could hear her office trolls muttering: "We told you this was a bad idea." It had never occurred to her that he might really like her. She said, "This is kind of new to me."

"Look, I know." Ian moved his hand from her leg, ran his fingers through his marginally receding hairline, and sighed. "My therapist has told me I'm not ready for a relationship. I still feel shitty about what I did to my ex-girlfriend. She got pregnant. I didn't want to be a father, so she got an abortion and now she won't talk to me. It's hard because she was my best friend, and I miss her. We had a lot

— 51 —

in common. We met at a Trekkie convention. I stayed with her longer than I stayed with anyone else."

"If you don't want to start a family, it's better not to." Valerie wriggled closer to him, and he smiled at her, looked relieved.

If someone Valerie didn't know had told her what Ian just had, she would have dismissed him as a prick. But he was lying next to her, naked, warm, and vulnerable, and this made her feel sympathetic towards him. At the same time, she felt corrupted.

Later, Valerie wished their relationship had ended after that first night. Instead, they continued to sleep together. The sex improved somewhat when she discovered that if she took a shower and then ordered him to lick her, he got off. She never did come with him, and she felt that, really, she was a lesbian. In a bit of role reversal, she insisted on keeping their relationship discreet, since she didn't want anyone to think she wasn't an out-and-proud dyke. Despite their discretion, Kim guessed what was going on and withdrew from Ian.

Ian told his best male friend about the affair. His friend congratulated him; he said, "I'm sure you're just the man to straighten her out." When Ian told Valerie this, she pretended to barf. She didn't want to meet this friend. Meanwhile, Ian wasn't any more comfortable in her world. When Valerie wound up with an extra ticket to see Ani DiFranco (Becky had cancelled), she emailed Ian to ask if he wanted to join her. He refused. It wasn't his scene. Didn't Ani DiFranco throw tampons at the audience or something?

The trolls cackled. "Bisexual is one thing. Bisocial is another."

After Valerie had been seeing Ian for a month, Becky called to say she was marrying William. They had been living together for three years but had decided to have a wedding now that Becky was pregnant.

Valerie was furious. "Do you expect me to congratulate you?"

"C'mon, Valerie, give it a break. Do you expect me not to get married because you're a dyke and aren't allowed to?"

Valerie paced back and forth with her portable phone clamped to her ear. "I don't see why not. It's like you're joining a country club that has a sign on the front lawn that says 'No Jews allowed.'"

Becky sighed. "I want our relationship to be taken seriously, and I don't want to fight with his family about it. They're Catholic, for Christ's sake. Maybe it isn't fair to you, but I'm doing this."

Valerie couldn't think of anything to say. She had always thought of her sister as a rebel because Becky had introduced her to pot and cool bands. Now she thought that perhaps her characterization had been superficial, based more on what their parents said about Becky.

"I also quit my job."

"Why? Do you think a married mother shouldn't be a phone-sex worker?"

"I think it's time for me to do something I don't hate."

The receiver cut out. Becky had hung up on her. Valerie pressed the talk button, planning to call her sister back to give her hell, but a beep on the line let her know that someone had just tried to call her. She checked her message. It was from Ian, asking her if she wanted to come over. Valerie decided to talk to Becky another time when they had both calmed down.

When she got to Ian's condo, they watched an *X-Files*

episode together. It was the first time they didn't fuck. When the show was over, Valerie told him about Becky's call.

He looked at her as if she were crazy. "I can't believe you wouldn't go to your sister's wedding because of politics."

"It's not politics—it's my life," Valerie said. "It would be different if she just had a commitment ceremony. But a wedding in a Catholic church?"

"But it's her wedding!" Ian said.

"Clearly you and I live in two different universes," Valerie snapped.

Ian cleared his throat. "Maybe we should go back to being friends."

"But we're not friends." Valerie zipped up a black sweatshirt that used to belong to her ex-girlfriend. Without the sexual attention Ian gave her, she realized there wasn't much between them. She read some of the same books he did, but that shared interest suddenly seemed as insubstantial as froth on a latte. She had given Ian a few lessons in oral sex, but otherwise he had no real interest in being educated about the reality of being a dyke. She regretted that she had not dumped him first.

Shortly after that, Valerie saw Kim wearing one of Ian's acrylic sweaters. Kim kept smiling at everyone as if she were in a cult. She emanated sex like a new perfume. Valerie found herself admiring Kim's breasts for the first time, and the trolls hissed at that. Valerie called Ian up to ask what was going on, and he confirmed that they were seeing each other.

"What the hell are you going to do?" Valerie scoffed.

"Marry her?"

He paused. "Maybe."

Valerie stopped speaking to him after that. Kim became nervous and tentative around her as if she were apologizing for stealing Valerie's boyfriend. That irritated Valerie even more. She was not really mad at either of them; she was mad at herself. She realized that part of the reason she had fucked Ian was to understand straight women, to not feel so different from them.

Several months later, Ian dumped Kim. Since they were not discreet about their relationship, everyone knew about the breakup. Kim stumbled around looking like a wounded deer. Ian asked Valerie to have a drink with him at the fern bar. Valerie suggested coffee at Starbucks instead. Ian looked disappointed, but he agreed. After work, Ian drove them to the nearest Starbucks, which was in one of those upscale neighbourhoods populated by plenty of expensively dressed women on the late side of thirty with kids. There were two sets of mothers with twins. Another woman had triplets. The effects of fertility treatments, Valerie surmised as she and Ian waited for their decaf cappuccinos. When the Starbucks barista announced their order was ready, Ian hastily manoeuvred them into a booth. He obviously wanted to have a serious talk. The topic, unsurprisingly, turned out to be Kim.

"I don't know what happened. I just couldn't sustain it." He jiggled his leg up and down.

Valerie sipped her cappuccino and refrained from clapping a hand on his leg. She wasn't interested in listening to him mull over his relationship with Kim. She was more interested in what having sex with Kim had been like. Did she enjoy her first time? Had he made her come? She was afraid to ask Ian: he would either be offended or, worse,

— 55 —

start conspiring for them to have a threesome.

Ian didn't drink his coffee. "She liked to go shopping. A lot. In some ways, I just couldn't relate to her. She was insecure about you. She thought maybe I would be happier with you, that I wouldn't get bored."

Valerie perked up. She realized he was poking around to see if she wanted to renew their relationship. Nothing could have interested her less, although she did like the feeling of having power over him. "Hmm."

Ian continued. "She doesn't have much experience with relationships, you know? It makes a difference. She reads but not as much as you do."

"She adores you." Valerie smiled unpleasantly. "I think you're perfect for each other."

Ian looked baffled, but he tilted his head and sipped his coffee.

Valerie knew he was smart enough to drop the topic of relationships. She would never play the last card in her hand: her strange attraction to Kim. Kim wasn't her type, and Valerie wasn't sure she even wanted to sleep with her. But Valerie would have liked to watch Ian have sex with Kim or, better still, direct him while he had sex with Kim.

This fantasy would never happen. In fact, it was something she only ever admitted to the trolls.

PART TWO

ARE YOU COMMITTED?
Montreal, 1989-1990

1.

Clara climbed over bundles of *The McGill Daily* to reach a
free computer terminal. The paper's office was in the base-
ment of the Student Union Building, so there was no natural light. The space was crammed: newspapers stacked on
the floor, couches, chairs, computer terminals, drafting tables. Just about everyone in the room, except her, was
smoking. Before sitting down, she handed an ashtray to
Tim, the news editor, who was waving a cigarette around
as he made a point to someone.

Clara was here to write up an interview she had just
conducted with an American journalist who had returned
to the United States after years of living in Central America.
The U. S. government wanted to deport the woman because
of her sympathetic portrayals of communism in Latin
America. A student group, the Friends of the Sandinistas,
had invited the journalist to McGill University to deliver a
lecture. But there was a problem with the interview. Or perhaps Clara was the problem: she didn't seem to know nearly
as much about history and politics as the other students
who worked at the *Daily*. Even the meaning of the words
the other students used—words like "colonization," "hege-

mony," and "deconstruction"—wasn't clear to her. She *was* a first-year student, but another *Daily* volunteer, Benjamin, was also in first year, and he seemed to speak the same language the others did. (Yesterday, he had told Clara he was an "anarcho-syndicalist," whatever that meant.)

With her notes in hand, Clara got up from her seat and went to knock on the door of the darkroom. She would ask Bruno for advice about the story. He was the photo editor at the *Daily* and her roommate.

From behind the door, Bruno called out, "What is it?"

"It's me, Clara. Can I speak to you for a moment?"

Bruno came out of the darkroom, pulling the door shut behind him. When Clara had first met Bruno a few weeks ago, she had classified him as Not Cute, largely because of the constellation of pimples on his face. His acne seemed alive, mushrooms growing on the trunk of a tree. But he wasn't unattractive really. He was her height—five foot seven—and also, like her, naturally thin. Their styles, however, were completely different. Whereas she was dressed in a freshly laundered pair of tight Levis with a pink T-shirt from Cotton Ginny, Bruno's tattered, ink-stained clothes were of no discernible brand. In fact, his big black shoes, dark, baggy trousers, and long-sleeved white shirt seemed to belong to a different era. If not for his black and green mohawk, he could have stepped out of a newsreel featuring men standing in a breadline during the Depression.

Bruno slouched against the door frame, hands tucked behind his back, the smell of photo chemicals rising from him. "What's up, Clara?"

"I interviewed the journalist Margaret Randall." Clara paused for a moment to look over her notes. "She called the U. S. trade embargo against Cuba oppressive. But she also slammed the proposed Canada-U. S. free trade agree-

ment. So I don't get it. Is restricting trade bad or good?"
Bruno was in his final year of a bachelor's degree in Economics. Last week he had run a photo in the *Daily* of graffiti that said, "Fuck Free Trade."

Bruno's eyebrows scissored together. "Well, it depends—"

Clara interrupted: "So my question's not stupid?"

Bruno shook his head, and Clara felt relieved. "Not at all. When looking at trade issues, you need to consider the operation of power, at how equal the so-called trading partners are and who benefits."

Clara tucked a strand of her long brown hair behind the arm of her glasses. "Oh. Okay. Thanks."

"No problem." Bruno glanced at the large clock on the wall. "You want to get supper at Basha with me and Mike? He should be here any minute now."

Clara shook her head. Going out to dinner was not something she could afford right now. "I've got too much work."

"Okay. How about if I meet you here at six and we head down to the march together?"

"Sure."

Bruno went back into the darkroom, while Clara made her way back to the computer. She sat down and reread her interview, trying to decide whether to take out the final quote or add more context to her story. Mike, who was the editor-in-chief of the *Daily* and her other roommate, had told her she had a knack for simplifying political issues for the average reader. She had sucked up the compliment, though she thought that what Mike saw as ability was simply the result of her being the "average reader." What had drawn her to the leftist *Daily* was more instinct than ideology. Her parents voted NDP, so she wasn't entirely out of touch with the politics of the *Daily*, but she had discovered that neither she nor her family had a political analysis. In fact, the only thing she could remember her taciturn father saying regarding his support for the NDP was: "I'll never vote for the businessmen's parties."

During Clara's first week of university, she had lived in residence, which she wasn't able to afford. The savings she brought to pay for residence turned out to cover one semester, not the entire year she budgeted for. It was her screw-up and not one she could fix easily. Her parents were paying her tuition and told her they didn't have any more money to give. Perhaps living in residence, which had been Clara's mother's suggestion, had been cheaper when she went to university. She told Clara, "It's a wonderful experience. You'll make lifelong friends." Well, it didn't take Clara more than a few days to realize that would never happen. The girls she met kept asking her, "Does this make me look fat?" It was a conversation she didn't want to have and not just because she was skinny. She loathed the self-hatred leaching out of them like toxic waste. If she had wanted to meet girls who cared only about what boys thought of their bodies, she could have stayed in Camrose, Alberta. The boys in residence were no better. At parties they took turns telling her stories about Stupid Things They Did When They Were Drunk, although she supposed back home it would have been Stupid Things They Did When They Were Drunk and Got on a Tractor. The whole reason she chose such a demanding school as McGill was to find intellectual life, but the students she met in residence never wanted to talk about what they were learning.

When Clara found out she could withdraw from residence and get most of her money back, she went to the *Daily*'s office to get a paper to check the classifieds for a room to rent. Living off-campus was supposed to be less expensive. The first thing she noticed upon entering the *Daily* office was the giant bedsheet hanging on the wall. Spray-painted on the sheet in big black letters were the words "The McGill Daily," and stencilled beneath this in tiny red letters was the motto: "We will act as agents of social change." She wasn't sure what this meant exactly, but the attitude of the spray-painted sign—rebellion—was easy enough to grasp, and it appealed to her.

The second thing Clara noticed was the cool-looking boy who stood in front of her, reading the *Daily*. His tall athletic build was slightly at odds with his black clothing and the dyed-black hair streaming down his back. He was quite attractive yet seemed accessible. In his pale, pudgy cheeks and John Lennon glasses, Clara glimpsed a lurking nerdiness. Before she could ask him where she could pick up a copy of the paper, he looked at her and said, "What's your definition of freedom?"

"Excuse me?" Had she heard right? Had she just met a student who cared about ideas and not about the easiest way to achieve a decent GPA while still consuming massive quantities of alcohol? Neat.

The boy repeated the question.

A fire licked at her brain, and she said, "Freedom is a place where no one gets hurt."

He dug a pen out of his pocket and, after folding up the paper, scribbled down her response in the margin. Then he looked at her again. "Are you here for the staff meeting?"

She blurted out, "I'm looking for a place to live. Someone told me the *Daily* has a classified section."

The boy's narrow dark eyes scooted over hers. "Coincidentally, I'm looking for a roommate." He stuck his hand out. "Mike Noble. Editor-in-chief of the *Daily*."

"Clara Stewart." She shook his hand. They had the same handshake—brief and not defensively strong. She saw that he was wearing black fingernail polish and wondered what that meant. Was he gay or just comfortable enough with himself not to care what other guys would say about him? Either possibility was a welcome change of pace from residence.

Mike flipped through the paper he was holding. When he reached the classified section, he circled one of the ads with his pen and then handed the paper to her.

Clara read the ad: "Room for rent at Beaudry metro in left-wing household. $130 plus utilities. No cats, no liberals."

The rent was cheap, and he seemed interesting. She looked at him. "Why is it bad to be liberal?" Where she came from people who hated liberals were conservatives, which he clearly was not.

"It means you're not committed."

"To what?"

Mike frowned, and Clara hoped he didn't regret showing her the ad. "To revolution, to the struggle, to change."

"Oh, I want the world to change," Clara hastened to reassure him. She wondered though, if what she meant was she wanted *her* world to change.

At six o'clock, Bruno returned to the *Daily* with Mike. Clara had filed her story about ten minutes earlier and grabbed a chocolate bar from a vending machine for dinner. She and Bruno were going to the Take Back the Night march, an annual event to protest violence against women. She would write a story on the march and Bruno would take photos.

Mike, Clara, and Bruno headed east along St. Catherine

Street past old, beautiful greystone buildings, many of which had garish signs in the windows advertising discounts on the cheap clothing or electronics sold inside. As they passed Place des Arts, a brigade of children wielding umbrellas nearly trampled them. It wasn't raining exactly, but now and then Clara would feel moisture on her face or hands, as though someone had spit on her. In a light sweater, she was slightly underdressed, so she hugged herself to keep warm. But then the wind subsided, and the colour of the sky shifted like a mood ring from grey to indigo.

Clara, who was walking behind Mike, touched the sleeve of his battered leather motorcycle jacket to get his attention. He immediately moved his arm out of reach. He wasn't a touchy-feely person. Students at the *Daily* who had grown up in Montreal, as Mike had, tended to greet people by kissing them on both cheeks, but Clara had noticed that Mike never did.

Now he inquired, "Did you want to ask me something?"

"I think the march is such a great idea that I don't think I can write about it with objectivity. Is that okay?"

Mike exhaled smoke. "Objectivity is bullshit."

Clara increased her stride to keep pace with Mike and Bruno. "What do you mean?"

Bruno turned his head to meet Clara's eyes. "Everything that's expressed is a political choice. Not taking a stand means you're confirming the status quo."

Mike added, "The model of objectivity is recent. Newspapers used to openly declare their political affiliations, but today they merely reflect the agendas of their corporate masters while pretending to be objective."

"I see," Clara said. She guessed this meant it was okay

for her to be as much participant as observer at the march, but shouldn't she put more in the story besides her own impressions? "Should I get quotes from other women?"

"Sure," Bruno said. "You might talk to the McGill Women's Union. I bet they'll be marching."

The McGill Women's Union was the feminist group on campus. Clara had dropped by the office once, but the door had been locked.

"As long as you don't mind getting the angry lesbian perspective," Mike put in.

Clara made a face. "Yeah, right. If you're a feminist, you're an angry lesbian." It was a sentiment she had heard growing up but not what she expected from Mike, who just shrugged in response. When he disagreed with Bruno, Mike wouldn't back down, but with Clara, he was more likely to drop the matter. She wasn't sure if he respected her less or was simply being polite. She hoped it was the latter. He *was* polite. Right now he was dropping his cigarette butt into a garbage can. He never littered and was tidier than either Clara or Bruno.

"Hey, we're here," Bruno announced pointlessly when they reached St. Denis Street. There was a considerable crowd of people, and Mike, after making plans to meet Clara and Bruno later, headed up an alley to avoid the throng. A woman stood at the front of the gathering on a small podium, giving a speech in French. Sign language interpreters translated it for the hearing impaired, their hands and fingers clenching and swooping a reel of meaning. Bruno took his camera out, focused the lens, and snapped a few shots. Then he and Clara went their separate ways. Men weren't allowed to march, although some men showed support by standing on the sidelines blowing whistles and holding up signs that said, "Men Against Violence Against Women."

The woman at the front finished her speech, and everyone around Clara began to clap, shout, cheer, and blow whistles. Some women on her right began chanting, "Women unite! Take back the night!" Then the march began with a forward lurch, heading up St. Denis Street, and Clara trudged along. Everyone was yelling slogans, but she felt too self-conscious to shout in public. What she felt like doing was reaching over to the nearest woman and hugging her. Being in a crowd of women chanting feminist slogans was both reassuring and exhilarating.

She made her way to the front of the march. After getting a pen and her notebook out of her knapsack, she began to take notes. She wrote down the words she saw on a banner: "*La rue, la nuit, femmes sans peur.*" What did "*peur*" mean? She made a mental note to check the word later in Bruno's French-English dictionary. Transcribing the words of a French chant—"*Quand une femme dit non, c'est non*"—she realized she did know what that meant: when a woman says no, that's no.

Yes, Clara thought. No is no, even if you hadn't minded at first when he touched you. Take back the night—she wanted to take back two weeks, two weeks of the summer she was twelve and her cousin Joey had done things to her he had no right to do. Fuck. She didn't want to think about that now: she had an article to write.

She scribbled notes about the women surging by her: an older woman who was walking with a cane, two mothers with babies strapped to their backs, and a woman riding a unicycle. The woman on the unicycle had short hair, except for a skinny braid that jumped across her back as she pedalled furiously. As Clara scribbled down descriptions of the marchers, four younger women carrying a banner that read "McGill Women's Union" passed by her.

Remembering Bruno's suggestion that she get a quote from them, Clara dashed after the women. When she caught up, she could hear them boisterously chanting, "Two-four-six-eight, no more violence, no more hate!" She felt awkward interrupting but reached forward anyway to tap the shoulder of the woman closest to her, a tall woman holding the end of the banner.

"Excuse me," Clara said. "Can I interview you?"

The woman stared. Her dark, wavy hair was worn in a very short style, cropped like a man's, except for two tiny spit curls beside her ears. Her high, round cheekbones and straight nose had the androgynous perfection of a model, whereas the fleshiness of her face and lips was indubitably feminine. She was, Clara thought, like one of those shimmering postcards that change depending on which direction you shift them in: woman, no, boy, no, woman.

"Interview me for what?" the woman demanded in a loud, nasal tone, bringing Clara back to the task at hand.

"*The McGill Daily.*"

The woman craned her neck in the direction of the other women holding the banner. "Can someone take the end?" she yelled.

Someone did, and the woman led Clara over to the curb where it was less crowded. Strewn along the gutters were leaves, a sodden mass of all the colours in a flame. In Alberta, there were no red or orange leaves, just yellow, but in Montreal, given the maple trees, fall was a full-colour spectrum.

The woman offered Clara a wry smile. "The *Daily*, huh? I didn't know they had any women on staff."

There were, in fact, very few women at the *Daily*, but Clara didn't appreciate being given attitude by a complete stranger. "Yeah, well, I've heard the Women's Union is made up of angry lesbians, but I've learned not to make assumptions."

"On the contrary, in my case, assume away." The woman regarded Clara with an expression that was somewhere between amusement and a dare.

Clara had never met a lesbian before—or at least anybody willing to admit to being one. She stammered, "C-c-can I quote you on that?"

The woman looked at her a little strangely. "If you want. The name's Gabby Miller. But I don't have time right now to do an interview. Can this wait for another day?"

Although the paper was called the *Daily*, it actually came out four times a week and included a French edition run by a separate staff. Since the French edition appeared tomorrow, Clara wouldn't have to file her story tonight. "I guess so. How's tomorrow?"

Gabby Miller frowned. "My schedule on Wednesdays is pretty crazy. Would interviewing me at five o'clock be too late?"

"No, that's cool."

"How about we meet at the Women's Union and then grab a coffee? Do you know where our office is?"

"I do," Clara said. She opened her notebook and scrawled down the time and place of her meeting with Gabby. As she was writing, Clara could feel Gabby looking at her.

Gabby said, "You didn't tell me your name."

"Oh. Sorry. I'm Clara Stewart." Clara stuck out her hand, and Gabby seized it in an energetic grip.

"Good to meet you."

Gabby released Clara's hand. Their business concluded, Clara expected Gabby to go back to her friends, but she lingered. The two of them stood together in a not uncomfortable silence, watching women march by. The wind twisted around them, sending the garbage on the street tumbling, and goosebumps arose on Clara's legs beneath her jeans. She rubbed her hands against her legs to warm them up, and Gabby, who noticed, said, "You're cold. We should get going."

"You go ahead," Clara said. "I'm going to take some more notes."

"Okay, see you tomorrow then."

While Clara put her pen and paper back into her knapsack, she watched Gabby swerve aggressively by the tight-faced cops guarding the rear of the march. Clara had stayed behind because Gabby felt like something she needed to digest. Gabby was a lesbian. Clara remembered being in junior high. There had been a girl, Jennifer Hill, that all the boys liked because she had a pretty body. Jennifer and her two best friends wore tight Jordache jeans and Cougar boots and screeched "lezzie" at all the girls they thought were uncool. When they yelled the word at Clara, it had felt like a gross bug she needed to squish. But now that she was in university, she didn't have to think of lesbians as disgusting.

After the march ended, Clara headed down to Foufounes. Although she and Bruno had agreed that meeting up after the march would be too difficult, they wound up bumping into each another. As they walked together along St. Catherine, they passed hookers dressed so boldly in their short skirts and thigh-high boots that Clara didn't have to think twice about what their profession was. During the march, one pair of working girls had raised their fists in solidarity with the women marching, and everyone had cheered. In downtown Edmonton, the street prostitutes were usually native girls in jeans, but in Montreal they were much more stylish. So were the panhandlers sitting in front of Foufounes. Young punks, with hair in primary colours spiked up like the crown on the Statue of Liberty, had their cups out, dangling for change, while a couple of large dogs with black collars slept beside them. The punks almost made being homeless seem like an alternative lifestyle.

Inside the bar, the English Beat was playing. Tuesdays were Ska Night. On the dance floor were a few guys wearing jeans with suspenders, their knees swinging up while their fists slammed down. It was just after ten, still early, and the place hadn't filled up yet. Clara and Bruno found Mike sitting at the bar with his girlfriend, Una, who was also the features editor of the *Daily*. Una and Mike, who were about the same height with matching pale skin, long dark hair, and black clothing, could pass for brother and sister, a spooky incestuous couple like characters in the trashy V. C. Andrews novels that Clara had read in junior high. And in fact, they bore the trapped, listless expressions of two people who had been locked away forever in an attic.

Clara sat down on an empty stool beside Mike. "You were right about the Women's Union," she told him.

"Yeah?" Mike didn't look at Clara. He was preoccupied by Una, who was scowling at him.

Clara swivelled back and forth on her bar stool. "I met someone from the Women's Union, and she was an angry lesbian." Except Gabby hadn't been angry exactly; Una was angry. Gabby had been fierce and composed and not entirely wrong about the *Daily*: the only woman to hold an editorial position was Una.

"Surprise, surprise." Mike reached past Clara to flick the ash of his cigarette into an ashtray. His arms were bare, and Clara noticed he had muscles—hard curlicues beneath soft skin she wanted to touch. She didn't have anything as drastic as a crush on Mike, although she wouldn't mind fooling around with him. But with Una in the picture, that wasn't going to happen.

"Clara!" It was Una, and her tone was sharp. "You're driving me crazy. Quit fidgeting."

Clara realized she was still spinning her stool back and forth. She stopped. Had Una noticed Clara checking out Mike, or was Una just being a pill? It was hard to tell. Una hung out with the two women who did the layout and design at the *Daily*, and although they were all polite enough to Clara, they never asked her to join them when they went out for coffee or a slice of pizza.

The bartender set a pitcher of beer in front of Bruno, who poured draft into two glasses and handed one to Clara.

"I don't have any money to give you," Clara protested.

"Don't worry about it."

Clara did worry but took the beer anyway. She needed a part-time job. The reality of Quebec being a French-speaking province hadn't sunk in until she had discovered that you had to be bilingual even to land a retail job at a mall. She had tried to find work on campus, but all the positions were sewn up, passed from one friend to another.

Bruno raised his glass to Clara, and they clinked glasses. Then he asked, "So who'd you meet from the Women's Union?"

"Gabby Miller."

"Don't think I know her."

Bruno was friendly with many of the organizations housed in the Student Union Building, but maybe lesbians were outside his social circle. Although the mandate of the *Daily* was to oppose racism, sexism, and homophobia, the staff was white, largely male, and, as far as Clara knew, heterosexual. After taking a swallow of her beer, she asked her roommates, "Is anybody at the *Daily* gay?"

Mike glanced at Bruno, who took a drag on his cigarette before announcing, "I've had my cock sucked by a guy or two."

Clara was surprised. Between Mike and Bruno, Clara would have selected Mike, with his long hair and black fingernail polish, as the one more likely to have had a homosexual experience. Even Una seemed startled by Bruno's statement. The sourness on her face was replaced by curiosity.

"But you think homosexuality is bourgeois decadence," Mike said to Bruno. "Now that you've decided you're a communist." (Mike, Clara knew, was an anarchist.)

"What I said," Bruno protested, "was that homosexuality was decadent for *me*. But it's no big secret. Sometimes getting a blow job's just getting a blow job."

Clara stared at her drink, so she wouldn't have to look at Bruno. Even though he was acting casual, he had made a vulnerable admission, and you didn't look at people when they did that. Did this mean Bruno went to the tiny parks in their neighbourhood and let strangers blow him? She had thought being homosexual was more like being an albino— genetic, rare, and obvious—not an activity a person could dabble in. She risked a glance at Bruno. "I thought homosexuality was genetic."

Bruno took one of Mike's cigarettes out of a pack he had left on the counter. "I don't see how. If homosexuality was genetic, that would disprove Darwin's theory of evolution."

Mike picked up his cigarettes and put them in his back pocket. Then he offered his opinion. "That's only if you assume homosexuality isn't the result of a mutation in a gene after fertilization."

Whereas Una was silent, Clara entered the fray of the boys' conversation, the nature versus nurture debate. Whenever she was late for class, it was usually because she had gotten sucked into a discussion with Mike and Bruno. She often thought she was learning as much from them as she was from her classes.

The day after the march, Clara woke up late. Bruno and Mike weren't around, but evidence of their morning routine was. The surface of the kitchen table was covered with empty cups of espresso, *The Globe and Mail* and *Le Devoir*, and half a dozen heavy glass ashtrays—they had been stolen from restaurants and bars—crammed with cigarette butts. She could empty the ashtrays but knew if she did so, it would become a daily chore. Bruno was supposed to tidy up the kitchen, but he was lax.

When Clara had moved in, Mike informed her that everyone was assigned certain responsibilities, tasks that came with titles half-pilfered from *1984*: Mike was the Minister of Plenty, which meant he collected money from the others to pay the bills and made sure the house was always stocked with toilet paper and cleaning supplies; Bruno was the Minister of the Interior and had to sweep and mop the floors of the communal rooms and keep them neat; and Clara would be the Minister of Health, which meant she was to take out the garbage and clean the bathroom. That she, the lone female, would be cleaning toilets struck her as dubious, but, apparently, the departing Minister of Health had been male. The bathroom itself was small, consisting of a toilet and an old claw-footed tub. There was no shower or sink, so one had to brush one's teeth using running water from the tub faucet. But after a few days, Clara didn't miss having a sink and was actually pleased to have one less thing to clean.

The phone rang. Clara picked up the receiver from the kitchen table. "Hello."

"Good afternoon, madam. I'm calling from the *Gazette*, and I wondered if you would be interested in a free trial subscription."

"No thanks." As Clara hung up, a thought occurred to her. Soliciting subscriptions to an English-language news-paper was something she could probably do without speaking French. She hated the idea of selling things to people, but at this point she was ready to take any job. The cost of living was so much more than she had imagined. She had to buy food and toothpaste and shampoo and a metro pass plus bedding, a pillow, and towels. Mike and Bruno's former roommate had left behind a futon, which had been conven-ient. For bookcases, Clara was using some milk crates that Bruno had looted early one morning from outside a depan-neur.

Today she needed money to take Gabby Miller out for coffee, so she hauled the dozens of cases of empty beer bottles in the kitchen to the dep.

Later that day, Clara went to meet Gabby. After climbing several flights of stairs, she stood in front of the open door-way of the Women's Union, trying to catch her breath. Then she entered a long, narrow room. Along one wall was a row of tall windows overlooking another building. Across from these windows, a small group of women was seated on chairs, cushions, and a ratty green couch. Gabby Miller wasn't among them, but an attractive, slender woman, who was sitting on a floor cushion with her legs folded like a yoga instructor, looked up at Clara.

"Hi, I'm Kirsten," the woman said. Kirsten was wearing an old blue housedress, and her long, black hair was twisted into ropes like a rag doll.

Clara introduced herself and asked if Gabby Miller was around.

Kirsten frowned. "You're not here for Bi the Way?"

"Excuse me?"

"This is the bisexual women's support group, and we're having a meeting," Kirsten explained.

Clara thought, Bisexuality? It was something she associated with David Bowie's Ziggy Stardust phase and porn movies. "I'm supposed to meet Gabby Miller here."

"I haven't seen Gabby today, but you can wait for her here if you like," Kirsten offered. She indicated an empty cushion beside the couch.

Clara sat down uncertainly and set her knapsack on the floor. Some of the other women in the room gave her tiny, welcoming smiles, which she nervously returned before looking around. On the wall behind the couch were three posters: a picture of peace doves; a drawing of a clenched fist encircled by a woman's symbol; and a photograph of two long-haired women in blue jeans holding hands and wearing purple T-shirts that said, "This is What Lesbians Look Like." The point seemed to be that lesbians looked like anyone else, and, indeed, the girls surrounding Clara didn't appear so different from the female students in her classes or in residence. Kirsten had a funkier style, but her dreadlocks and second-hand dress didn't detract from her prettiness so much as throw it into sharp relief.

A ponytailed blonde wearing a full-length fur coat entered the room.

"Is that beaver?" Kirsten asked in an incredulous tone.

"It's cold up here in Canada," the girl said, speaking with an unmistakable Deep South twang. She raised her palms at Kirsten. "I know. People stop me on the street to tell me these coats are illegal and that the beaver is your national animal, but don't y'all have a statute of limitations on these things? This coat was my grandmother's. These beavers have been dead for at least fifty years!"

"I suppose my Doc Martens are leather," Kirsten said, and Clara noticed that Kirsten was wearing purple Doc Martens boots with red laces.

The blonde tossed her heavy coat on a table where other coats were piled up. Then she sat down on the last remaining cushion, which was beside Clara. She looked over at her. "Hi there."

"Hi."

The girl moved closer to Clara and began speaking in a low, rapid tone. "I can't believe I'm here. My father always told me never to join a group, never to give out my name and number to any organization. But I came because I've never dated a boy. I always just thought I was a good Christian girl, but the truth is I'm not interested." She paused to take a breath. "How about you?"

Uh oh. The girl was trying to bond with Clara, or maybe even flirt. Clara drew her body back. "I'm not here for the meeting. I'm just waiting for someone."

The girl flushed. "I see."

Clara, who couldn't think of a way to dispel the awkwardness, turned around and began to scrutinize the titles of the books on the large bookshelf behind them. There were novels by Amy Tan and Toni Morrison and Alice Walker along with feminist classics by Betty Friedan and Germaine Greer. A title Clara had never heard of caught her attention: *Pleasure and Danger.* She was about to take the book from the shelf when she heard Kirsten ask everyone to be quiet.

Clara faced the group again. Kirsten, after waiting for everyone's full attention, began to speak. "First of all, I'd like to remind people that next week we'll meet at our regular time and space at Concordia University. By then, the painting will be finished, and hopefully those women with sensitivities to the fumes will be able to cope. Second, since there are some new faces here, let's go around the circle and introduce ourselves. I'm Kirsten, I'm a Concordia student, and, as most of you know, I'm the coordinator of this group."

One by one the dozen women around Clara offered their first names to the group. When it was Clara's turn, she introduced herself, adding hesitantly, "I just happen to be hanging out here if that's okay."

No one protested. Then the blond American, the only woman left to introduce herself, said, "I'm Monica. I've never been to one of these meetings, but I heard that being in the closet was tonight's topic, and I'm farther in the closet than the dustballs."

There was a moment of silence. Some members looked expectantly at Kirsten, who, after a beat, said, "Thanks for sharing that, Monica." Kirsten paused. "Um, what I want to talk about is how bisexuality is a two-way closet. In the summer, I suggested that the group march at Pride, but people were reluctant."

A girl in overalls immediately spoke up, as if Kirsten's remark had been directed at her: "I'm afraid if I come out as bi, lesbians in the community won't want to date me."

Kirsten nodded solemnly. "I've had that reaction. A few months ago, I had a lesbian tell me I could give her a disease. But I did march at Pride this summer with a 'Bi Pride'

T-shirt I made myself, and a lot of women came up to me to say they were bi."

Monica, who was staring intently at Kirsten, interrupted. "Did you always know that about yourself, that you're attracted to both sexes?"

Kirsten gave a little laugh. "Not at all. In fact, it never occurred to me to date girls until last year." When a few of the women looked as puzzled as Clara felt, Kirsten explained. "I had a friend who wanted to go to a lesbian bar, and I decided to tag along for the hell of it. But then I met a woman, and we went back to my place and had sex. The next morning, I broke up with the guy I'd been seeing to go out with her."

Clara struggled to take in this information. Last night, Bruno had talked about having homosexual experiences, and now Kirsten was describing going into a bar and turning bisexual. Could that happen to Clara?

Another woman grinned at Kirsten. "That girl you picked up must have been really something in the sack."

Kirsten blushed, and everyone laughed, including Clara. She wondered if it was possible to join Bi the Way even though she wasn't bisexual. These women seemed nice, and she didn't really have any female friends. For some reason, she tended to get along better with guys. In high school, she had hung out with a few girls, who had dropped her for being a slut, for making out with different boys all the time, something Clara did more out of boredom than passion. She had been baffled by the attitude of her so-called friends. None of the boys in their gang were given a hard time for fooling around, or trying to, with various girls. She supposed that the girls were upset with her mainly for rejecting one of the guys they hung out with, a boy who had genuinely liked her. He had been sweet, but, God, he couldn't kiss at all. One night he had looked into her eyes, picked up her hands, and said reverently, "Your little white hands." It was so corny that Clara had wanted to puke on the spot. He kept doing that, handing her his feelings the way you passed someone the salt at the table, as though it were natural and ordinary for him to say he cared about her. His behaviour had made her so uncomfortable, partly because she didn't feel the same way and partly because her own feelings were like a wounded animal that would die of exposure if brought out into the open. No one in her family ever talked about feelings.

The door of the Women's Union banged open, and Gabby Miller strode in. "Oy, I know, I'm late," Gabby said loudly as she marched up to Clara, oblivious to the meeting she was interrupting. Clara slipped her knapsack over her shoulder and stood. Everyone stared, and Kirsten, who had been talking, stopped.

Clara said, "Excuse me, but I have to go. It was nice to meet you guys."

Kirsten said, "You can come back if you want." She looked at Gabby. "Thanks, Gabby, for loaning us the space."

Gabby smirked. "Always happy to help Bi on the Way!"

A girl asked, "Isn't it Bi the Way?"

Kirsten sighed. "Gabby's being cute. She's trying to say bisexuality is a pit stop on the way to being a lesbian. Maybe that was the case for Gabby, but that's not true for all of us."

"Right. As if I ever considered myself bi." Gabby rolled her eyes. Then she walked out of the room, and Clara reluctantly followed. Gabby seemed to have strong feelings about things. Clara would probably get some good quotes from her, although she wasn't sure she would enjoy coffee with this woman. People in Montreal seemed so sure of themselves, and Clara couldn't decide whether she envied them for it or disliked them because of it. When they reached the bottom of the stairs, Gabby suggested they do the interview in the student lounge, across from the *Daily*, and Clara agreed. She would be going back to the *Daily* afterwards to file the story.

They walked into the dark, smoky student lounge, Gabby leading the way. There was an empty table at the back, and the two of them sat down. Gabby sat with her feet planted firmly apart and her elbows on the table. In contrast, Clara tucked her elbows in and twisted her legs and feet around each other. A waitress came and took their orders for two bowls of café au lait.

After the waitress left, Clara took a pen and some paper out of her knapsack. As she was doing so, Bruno caught her eye and waved on his way out of the lounge.

Gabby said, "One of the *Daily* guys, I suppose."

"Bruno? Yeah, but he's also my roommate."

"You're kidding!" Gabby shook her head. "Nice terrorist chic."

"What are you talking about?"

Gabby raised her eyebrows. "The *keffiyeh* he's wearing?"

When Clara continued to look blankly at her, Gabby said, "His Palestinian support scarf."

"Oh." Clara supposed Gabby must mean the long black-and-white scarf with the little round fringes Bruno had begun draping around his neck and over his collarbone now that the weather was chillier. The scarf had looked ethnic to Clara, but she hadn't known the origin.

"I'm not stupid," Gabby said doggedly, as though Clara had accused her of this. "I know it's complicated. But can we not have a conversation about Palestine?"

"Sure," Clara said. She was still trying to absorb enough

facts about the Middle East to have an opinion.

Their bowls of coffee arrived. While Gabby dumped in packets of sugar, which remained suspended for a few seconds on the froth, Clara stared at the men's shirt Gabby was wearing with black jeans. On another woman, a men's shirt would have been sloppy, the sort of thing Clara might wear to help her mother in the garden, but on Gabby the white shirt seemed dressy, maybe because both her shirt and pants were ironed. An iron was one of the many ordinary household items Clara and her roommates did without. But, she wondered, was that because they couldn't afford an iron, or because they mostly wore T-shirts, or because ironing was bourgeois? It was hard to tell sometimes what was political and what was personal.

"So." Gabby stared at Clara. "What do you want to know?"

Clara picked up her pen. "I guess my first question is, why did the Women's Union participate in the march?"

"I can't speak for other women, only for myself," Gabby said. "But I marched because safety is an issue that affects all women. In the spring, an investment banker was gang-raped while jogging in Central Park in New York. If it could happen to her, it could happen to anyone."

Clara jotted down the quote. "Gee, I'd forgotten about that."

"There are lots of reasons for marching." Gabby began to reel off statistics, tapping her forefinger against the fingers on her other hand with each new piece of data she offered Clara: the percentage of women in the population who were victims of domestic violence, the percentage of women who were raped, the number of rapes that occurred in a year, prosecution and conviction rates for sexual assault and domestic violence.

Clara frantically made notes. When she had finished, she said, "How do you know all this?"

"It's my job. I'm one of the coordinators of the Women's Union this year."

"Do you think the march should exclude men?" Clara wasn't sure how she felt about this or the fact that men were barred from the Women's Union.

"Yes, it's entirely appropriate." Gabby spoke firmly. "Violence is perpetrated by men, not women."

Clara put her pen down and stared at Gabby. "But if men are the problem, don't they need to be part of the solution?"

"Since I'm a lesbian, men aren't part of my solution."

"I see." Clara wasn't sure whether to admire Gabby for being so assertive about her lesbianism or whether she, Clara, should feel put down for being heterosexual.

When Clara didn't say anything else, Gabby asked, "Is that it?"

"Pretty much." Clara sipped her rapidly cooling coffee, while Gabby fiddled with a napkin.

"Is this the only story you're working on?" Gabby asked. She sounded less confident all of a sudden, as though she had picked up on Clara's ambivalence towards her.

"Well, Mike—he's the editor of the *Daily* and another one of my roommates—"

Gabby interrupted Clara, "You live with Mike Noble?"

"Do you know him?"

"Who doesn't?" Gabby rolled her eyes again. "Big radical dick on campus."

Clara tried to decide whether this was as offensive as Mike calling the Women's Union angry lesbians. Oddly enough, Gabby and Mike reminded Clara of each other:

both of them liked to throw down the gauntlet. Clara decided to ignore Gabby's comment, however. "Mike asked me to do a piece on East Timor for our issue on liberation armies."

Gabby, who was taking a sip of coffee, almost choked. When she recovered, she said angrily, "Liberation armies? What does that mean? Don't tell me the *Daily* is writing about terrorist groups like the PLO?"

Clara didn't see any point in denying what would soon be public knowledge. Bracing herself for more outrage, she said, "Yup. If it makes a difference, the guy writing about the PLO is Jewish."

Gabby laid her arms flat on the table and, looking Clara in the eye, spoke emphatically: "Armies. Could the *Daily* be more patriarchal? You're writing about the Take Back the Night march, so I assume you're at least sympathetic to feminism and issues of violence. Why don't *you* write about the feminist peace movement?"

Clara held Gabby's gaze. In a calm tone, she said, "That's not a bad idea. Especially since I don't even know where frigging East Timor is."

Gabby leaned back in her chair. She wasn't smiling, but there was something close to satisfaction on her face, as though she had won this round. When the waitress dropped off the bill, she snatched it before Clara could. Gabby put five dollars on the table to cover both of their coffees.

It meant one thing when a man paid the bill, but, what, Clara wondered, did it mean when a woman did? Should she clarify her heterosexuality to Gabby? No, that would sound stupid.

Clara said, "I was going to pay since you let me interview you."

Gabby dismissively waved her hand. "Next time," she

said, as though they might do this again. She stood up. "I should get going. I have an essay to finish for tomorrow. Where are you headed?"

"To the *Daily*." Clara stood, too.

"See you later then," Gabby said. She leaned towards Clara to kiss her on both cheeks, but Clara was still so unused to this Montreal kissing ritual that she simply gave Gabby a quick hug. It was awkward, yet the fact that the hug seemed uncomfortable for both of them pleased Clara. Maybe she wasn't the only one who felt self-conscious sometimes. Clara also realized there was another reason Gabby reminded her of Mike: Clara felt the same way about both of them, a mixture of interested and annoyed.

2.

On a Friday evening in early November, Clara strode quickly up the long escalator in Beaudry metro station. She and her roommates were throwing a party tonight, and she needed to get ready. She was coming back from work and was running late. Getting a telemarketing job at the *Gazette* had turned out to be easy. The job was available only part-time and didn't pay well. Employees had the option of being paid either minimum wage (provided they made one sale an hour) or a commission. Only one employee opted for a commission: Walker, a black teenager living in the projects of Little Burgundy, whose modus operandi was to use the same last name as the person he was calling. "We have the same last name!" he would say. "Man, what a co-incidence." Walker, who had trained Clara, encouraged her to borrow his cheesy technique. She had tried it tonight, and it did result in higher sales, but lying to people and then bonding with them over the lie felt too uncomfortable. She was glad, though, to have a job that brought in enough money to live on. As a result, she wouldn't have to resort to student loans, at least for this semester.

As Clara left the metro, she passed a group of dark-haired men with moustaches laughing and joking in French. They were probably gay. Her apartment was a few blocks from the Gay Village, a noisy strip of late-night bars and diners. Walking through the strip on her way home at night felt safe: the men were interested in one another, not her.

She walked north, out of the Village. Moisture brushed her cheeks, and she realized it was beginning to snow—wet snow that dissolved almost immediately against her wool coat. At Maisonneuve Street, she went into a fruit and vegetable market and picked up beer, three large bags of chips, a container of sour cream, and a packet of French onion soup mix. Outside the store, the handles of the flimsy plastic bags she was carrying bit into her cold, bare fingers, but she didn't have far to go. At the end of the block, she reached her building, a greystone duplex built at the beginning of the century. Spray-painted across the front door were the words "*À bas l'État,*" which Bruno had to explain meant "Down with the State."

Inside the apartment, Clara found Mike energetically sweeping the kitchen floor. She stowed her beer in the fridge and began putting the chips in bowls and preparing the dip by combining the onion soup mix with the sour cream.

"Want a contribution?" Mike asked.

"Sure," Clara said, a little surprised.

He handed her a few dollars. "You might not want all that beer. Mathieu's bringing some shrooms. Since we're hosting the party, we get a discount: five dollars a gram."

"Cool." Clara tried to sound nonchalant. She had never taken shrooms or any drugs besides pot, not so much for lack of interest as lack of availability. Back in Alberta, she and her friends mostly just drank bottles of rum or vodka purchased by older siblings and former babysitters. But here

— 90 —

in Montreal, the clubs were full of drugs. In the washrooms at Foufounes, people snorted coke and PCP. Sometimes they even did drugs right on the dance floor. But drugs cost money. Half the time she was so broke, she snuck bottles of beer into her knapsack when she went to Foufounes.

Bruno emerged from his room and lit a cigarette. Then he grabbed some paper towels and, between drags on his cigarette, began to ineffectually dab at the burnt crusts of food stuck to the stove burners.

"I think I need a scrub brush, but we don't have one," Bruno said. "Is there something else I can use for cleaning?"

"There's a washcloth," Mike said. He set down the broom he was holding and went over to the sink, which was full of dishes. As he moved a stack of plates to get the rag, a glass cracked. Mike gave Bruno a peevish look. "Do you think you could do your dishes once in a while?"

"I do. I just don't wash them every day."

"No, you don't," Mike retorted. "You wait until you've used up every last mug and plate in the house."

"If you want to clean up after me, that's your bourgeois hang-up." Stubbing out his cigarette, Bruno stormed into his room, slamming the door. Mike went over to the record player in the living room and turned off Minor Threat.

"Fuck Bruno," Mike said.

"Aw, you don't mean that," Clara said. She wondered if Mike was on edge because Una had dumped him last week. She picked up a bowl of chips and the dip and thrust them in front of Mike. "Try the dip."

"Not right now."

Clara stuck her own finger in the dip and licked it. Her mom always made this dip for parties, and it was as good as she remembered. But she put it down and began to help

— 91 —

Mike clean up. After they finished, Clara took a bath. She was scrubbing herself dry with a towel when she heard the doorbell ring. According to the new clock in her bedroom, it was only five after ten. Their invitations had said, "Come after ten," and Clara had banked on no one showing up until at least ten-thirty. But by ten-thirty, she had raced downstairs four times to open the door to what was now heavy snow and groups of guys and girls jostling to come in from the cold. Clara didn't know the names of any of the guests but recognized many of their faces. They were mostly students involved in organizations that either had an office at the Student Union Building or used another group's office for their meetings. They were students who, as the *Daily* staff put it, weren't "apathetic."

"Good story on Margaret Randall," a girl with braids said as Clara led her and her friends into Bruno's room to stash their coats.

"Thanks," Clara said, suddenly realizing that she was talking to the Friends of the Sandinistas, who met at the *Daily* on Sunday nights. The members of this group circulated petitions and raised money to send farm equipment to Nicaragua, and they had all arrived at the party wearing alpaca sweaters.

"Is this your room?" one of the guys asked Clara, looking at the ceilings and walls, which were painted black. Spray-painted across one wall in crimson letters were the words "*Vivre libre ou mourir.*"

"Uh, no. This is Bruno's room."

The girl with the braid pointed to the graffiti. "What's that say?"

"Live free or die," Clara said. "It's his philosophy and also a song by Bérurier Noir."

"Cool."

Clara drifted into the kitchen where Mike was refilling the bowls with chips. Although Bruno's room had the most dramatic paint job, the rooms in the rest of the apartment weren't exactly nondescript. The ceilings and crown mouldings in the kitchen and living room—which were actually one large double room separated by an interior arch—were the shade of stewed prunes. The walls and baseboards of each portion of the room were different colours: mustard in the kitchen, olive in the living room. When Clara had first moved in, she had found the colours strange but now liked them.

Mike didn't seem to need any help, so Clara went into the living room, where she saw a light-skinned black guy with long, thin braids playing deejay. She knew his name—Lionel Hamilton—because he announced it often enough on his reggae show at CKUT, the campus radio station housed directly across from the *Daily*.

The doorbell rang again. Clara clomped down the stairs and let in some students from the *Daily*. Among them were Una's friends, but they had come without Una, which Clara suspected Mike would be happy about. Before Clara could show the *Daily* staffers where to put their coats, the doorbell sounded again. Soon every room in the apartment was full of people sitting on futons or the floor, drinking bottles of beer, and smoking cigarettes or dope. Some of the guests were as punk as Bruno or as goth as Mike. Others were more understated with only a nose stud or *keffiyeh* or long, black dirndl skirt to signify their anti-oppression stance. In Clara's own room, she found people sitting on her futon discussing the fall of the Berlin Wall. Bruno was at the centre of the discussion, and she heard him say, "Freedom to shop doesn't equal freedom from tyranny and oppression." She didn't feel she had much to contribute, and being around so many strangers made her shy. She had been taking refuge in the role of greeter, but it was midnight and the stream of guests coming in had slowed down. But then, a few minutes later, the doorbell rang again.

It was another *Daily* staffer, Mathieu. She told him, "People have been waiting for you."

"I bet," Mathieu said as he stamped the slushy snow from his hiking boots. With his shaggy hair and tight jeans, he looked more like the boys Clara had grown up with in Camrose. He was fairly apolitical for someone who worked at the *Daily*. He did the sports stories in both French and English (most student newspapers, Clara had learned, had sports editors, but no such position existed at the *Daily*, which rarely dedicated more than one story an issue to sports). Mathieu also sold pot to anyone who wanted it. He handed Clara a little plastic baggie with dried and shrivelled objects that she supposed were shrooms. "Ladies first."

"Thanks," Clara said. "I'll get you some money."

After she paid him, she went into the kitchen and opened a beer. She sat down at the kitchen table and used the beer to swallow the sour-tasting drugs. Before long, she felt a little nauseated. Then she started to get high. It was softer than being wasted; she could walk in a straight line. Only her mind was, as Mike put it, trippy.

Clara wandered through the party with a beer bottle in hand, staring dreamily at the bumps and fractures in the old plaster and lath walls, lines that revealed several layers of paint, which represented the lives of so many different people. She felt exquisitely attentive to her surroundings and her senses. The smells in each room filled her nostrils—sweat, sandalwood, the sleeves of damp wool sweaters, beer, cigarettes, salt and vinegar chips—and the beats from various styles of music flowed into her ears. A few guys were taking turns playing deejay, so one minute guests were crunching up their torsos and kicking out their feet to the Cramps, and the next they were swaying to Bob Marley's "Buffalo Soldier." A song came on that Clara hadn't heard before but liked immediately. The band was somewhere between rock and punk with a woman singer whose howling voice sank into Clara like teeth. One of Bruno's friends from Foufounes was hovering over the turntable, and she asked him who the singer was.

"*Quoi?*" he said.

"*La musique. La chanteuse.*" Nouns were manageable for Clara.

"*C'est Patti Smith.*" He handed her an album cover with a picture of a woman in a white dress holding a bird in her hand. He added, "Sorry. My English not so good."

Clara replied, as she had learned to in these situations, "*Pas de problème.*"

A girl in striped pants got up from the living room floor and began dancing by herself, smearing her hands around like a mime, and Clara left the boy to join her. The shrooms made Clara feel as though she were one with the music, not merely dancing but engaging in a primitive, tribal act. Her body moved of its own accord like a charmed snake.

Shortly after she started dancing, she saw a familiar-looking woman walk into the room. After a moment, Clara recognized her as Kirsten, the coordinator of Bi the Way. Kirsten didn't seem to know anybody but didn't look bothered by this. She appeared confident and self-assured, even though she was wearing a sleeveless, black velvet dress that showed that she wasn't wearing a bra and that her underarms weren't shaved. The nest of dark underarm hair would have been ugly on someone less appealing, but, on Kirsten, Clara thought it seemed obscene in a way that was somehow interesting, like watching a beautiful girl stick out her tongue. Kirsten's bare arms also revealed a tattoo, a black and red yin-yang symbol on her shoulder, just above her biceps. It had never occurred to Clara to get a tattoo before, but suddenly she wanted one. Kirsten managed to be tough and cool and girly all at the same time. She had a sophistication Clara wished she could rub over herself like musk.

Clara approached Kirsten. "Hey, what are you doing here?"

Kirsten looked a little taken aback. "Do I know you?"

"I came to a Bi the Way meeting once," Clara explained. "Not on purpose. I was meeting Gabby Miller at the McGill Women's Union."

"I remember now," Kirsten said. "How is Gabby these days?"

Clara hadn't seen Gabby since they had had coffee. "I don't know. We don't hang out."

Neither of them said anything for a moment. Then Kirsten asked, "Have you seen Mike around? He's the guy having this party."

Clara could have told Kirsten that she, Clara, was also hosting the party. Instead she said, "Not in the last little while. How do you know Mike?"

A trace of what looked like embarrassment flitted across Kirsten's face. "We used to go out."

Clara wondered if Mike had been the boyfriend whom Kirsten had dumped for a woman. But even stoned, she knew not to ask that particular question. Instead, she gestured towards Kirsten's arm and said, "Neat tattoo."

"Thanks," Kirsten said. "I got it while teaching English in Japan. You have to be a real outcast there to get a tattoo. Usually only the yakuza, that's the Japanese mafia, get tattoos."

"Does your tattoo symbolize anything?"

"It reminds me that the universe is both relative and interdependent. *Li* and *shih*. I follow the Kegon school of Buddhism."

Clara had no idea what Kirsten meant by any of this, although it sounded profound. "But you're not, like, from Japan?"

"No. I grew up in the B.C. Interior. My dad's a logger." Kirsten paused to inhale her cigarette. "I have a different background from the McGill kids here."

"Me, too, although I go to McGill," said Clara.

But Kirsten didn't seem all that interested. "Oh yeah. Who do you know here?"

"I live here," Clara replied.

"Really?" Kirsten's eyes sharpened and focused on Clara in a new way. "And you don't know where Mike is?"

Clara shrugged. "We can look for him." She led Kirsten out of the living room and into Mike's bedroom, but he wasn't there. He wasn't in Bruno's room either. She finally found him in her room, examining her cassette collection, which was in alphabetical order from Abba to the Velvet Underground. She liked rock and disco. Mike didn't have much in the way of music—he had everything Nick Cave had ever done and that was about it—but his lack of interest in music didn't prevent him from having opinions on Clara's and Bruno's music, and Mike's opinions tended to be snide.

Kirsten stood in the doorway, looking uncertain for the first time. Clara flopped down on an empty space on her futon, next to a guy and a girl who were stroking each other's faces. Her own high, she realized, had worn off. She listened to Kirsten and Mike exchange updates on their lives. The way they spoke was enthusiastic, yet other, less friendly emotions edged into the tones of their voices.

Kirsten was saying, "So I'm starting this band with two women. It's going to be really cool."

"Yeah? What are you called?"

"We don't have a rehearsal space yet, so I think it's a little premature to give ourselves a name. But the drummer is amazing. She's got these huge arms"—Kirsten leaned over to grip Mike's biceps, and Clara noticed Mike didn't move away—"and she just whacks on the drums, like she's chopping down trees with an axe."

"Maybe you should call yourselves the Lizzie Borden Band," Mike suggested.

Clara lifted her head from her pillow. "Too obvious. The Lizzie Borden Trio would be better."

Mike laughed. Kirsten did not. The couple sitting on Clara's bed stood up and left the room.

"The Lizzie Borden Band sounds punk and I hate punk," Kirsten said. There was something intense and emphatic about the way she said this, as though she really hated something or someone else. She lifted her dreads so that they hung over her back rather than her shoulders. "Anyway, I just thought I'd drop by and say hi."

"And now you have," Mike said.

"Say hello to Una."

Mike cleared his throat. "We're not together anymore."

"I see." Kirsten's eyes shifted speculatively to Clara. "Well then, don't say hello to Una."

Kirsten left the room, and Mike came over and lay on the bed beside Clara. It had never occurred to Clara that Mike might be attracted to her. But the way Kirsten had looked at Clara, the way Mike was now lying beside her, told her he was interested. Clara wished she could just let this information roll around, could stare at it as if it were a pretty coloured marble, but instead she had to make a decision. She was attracted to him, but they were roommates. Often after she had sex with a guy, she would avoid him, but that wouldn't be possible with Mike.

Mike looked at Clara, who looked away. But when he experimentally pressed his thigh against hers, she let him. When he didn't do anything else, she felt a whoosh of wanting and inevitability, so she crawled on top of him and kissed him. Their tongues touched for a moment, and he got up and shut the door. He lay back down with his eyes closed, as though waiting for her to get back on top of him. She complied but didn't kiss him—instead she stared at his long hair spilled like a girl's across her pillow. She had never slept with a boy who had long hair.

"Why do you paint your fingernails?" she asked. It was something she had always wanted to know, and it was the first time she felt close enough to him to ask.

"I just like it, okay?"

There was a shrill edge to Mike's tone, and Clara decided to respect his privacy, to not do the mean older-sister thing of making him tell her. Besides, it was a rare pleasure to see Mike vulnerable. He was one of those people who seemed perpetually in control.

Clara started kissing Mike. They made out for a while, kissing and rubbing against each other. Periodically, Mike would remove an item of Clara's clothing, then an item of his clothing. When they were finally both naked, Mike slid his hand between Clara's legs and touched her with different motions, experimenting with circles, rubbing, and up-and-down strokes. This was new for her. Usually guys didn't bother to try to please her or made rather feeble attempts. Sensation swam through her, but she also felt shy, vulnerable, so she shifted the focus to him, put her hand on his hard-on, and stroked him. When he came, she felt smug.

Afterwards, they lay on their backs, their shoulders touching, and Clara realized the party had ended. It was quiet, and light was no longer flooding beneath her bedroom door.

Mike mumbled, "You know I just broke up with Una."

God, Clara thought, now he would tell her he wasn't ready for a relationship. Why was he starting this conversation? It was unnecessary and embarrassing for both of them. Didn't he know better? But all she said was, "Uh huh."

Mike continued primly, "That's why I didn't fuck you."

Clara almost laughed. How could it not occur to Mike that she was just as happy not to have intercourse, not to worry about birth control and safe sex?

He added, "I didn't want to make you feel cheap."

Clara sat up, dragging the sheet with her so it covered her breasts, annoyance overriding her amusement. He didn't want to make her feel cheap? His line could have come from a bad romance novel, except the situation she was in seemed smaller and sourer than that. "You didn't."

Even Mike could read the irritation in her voice. "So, we're okay?"

They had been good, until he had started acting so serious. "Mike, we're roommates, and I gave you a hand job. It's not a big deal."

Mike blushed. Why he was blushing wasn't clear to Clara, but she didn't care. She just wanted him to leave. She hunkered down into her blankets, while he put his clothes back on and crept out of her bedroom.

A week after the party, Clara sat at the kitchen table typing an essay on her electric typewriter. The essay was a textual analysis of *A Hero of Our Time* for her favourite class, Russian Literature in Translation.

Shit. Clara had made another typo. She brushed white-out over the misspelled word but didn't manage to dab it in the right spot because the kitchen table was wobbly. The pine table was from Ikea and designed for two people, although four mismatched chairs were jammed around it, the largest of which Clara had tacitly claimed, even though in theory her roommates didn't believe in private property.

While Clara cursed and typed, Mike wandered into the adjoining living room with a white cloth and a bottle of nail polish remover. He dabbed the liquid onto the cloth and began rubbing the black from his fingernails, releasing a harsh chemical smell. Bruno came out of his bedroom and asked Mike if he was having dinner with his folks.

"Yup," Mike said.

"That's too bad," Clara said. "I was going to make a curry for everyone." A former roommate had left an Indian vegetarian cookbook behind.

"Sorry about that," Mike said.

He was in polite, retreat mode around Clara, and she didn't know how to get him to chill out. The whole situation was so stupid. Sometimes she wondered why she even bothered with sex at all.

After Mike left, Clara set her essay aside and began to prepare supper. As she washed spinach and peeled potatoes, she thought about Mike and how little she knew about him. Having sex had made them less rather than more intimate. Had he taken off his nail polish because his father might beat him up? If Clara's dad saw her brothers wearing nail polish, he would just make fun of them, but she could see some of her uncles, the ones who hadn't finished high school and drank a lot, doing much worse.

Clara turned to Bruno, who sat at the kitchen table smoking a cigarette, and asked, "Are Mike's parents really redneck?"

Bruno, who was in the middle of exhaling, started laughing, which caused him to choke. Clara handed him a glass of water but, after he sipped it and stopped coughing, he started laughing again.

"What's so funny?" Clara demanded.

"Mike's parents are psychiatrists who live in Westmount."

"What?" Clara was shocked. Even though she hadn't lived in Montreal long, she was aware that Westmount was the city's wealthiest—and traditionally English—neighbourhood. She had assumed Mike was a champion of the working classes because that was the background he came from.

"Surprise, surprise."

Clara asked, "So how come Mike took off his nail polish before going to see them?"

"Probably so he doesn't jeopardize his allowance. As long as he makes an occasional appearance for dinner, they give him seven hundred bucks a month."

Clara nodded, trying to take this in. She had assumed that Mike was able to pay his bills because of his job as editor-in-chief of the *Daily*. But come to think of it, just the other day he had remarked upon how meagre the honorariums were for the *Daily* staff.

"I thought you knew Mike better. Thought you knew him a whole lot better," Bruno said with an unmistakable leer.

My God. She thought she and Mike had been discreet, or at any rate she thought since Bruno hadn't mentioned anything that he didn't know. Maybe everyone at the *Daily* knew. Clara broke out in a sweat—this was one of those times when she regretted her recent decision to abandon antiperspirant for herbal deodorant. Her face felt as if she'd stuck it into a furnace. She couldn't look at Bruno. Finally she said, "Did Mike tell you?"

"I think Mathieu almost walked in on you guys or something. Mike, in case you haven't noticed, isn't big on talking about his emotional life. Maybe because his parents are psychiatrists."

"Hmm." Clara turned away from Bruno to check the rice. It was done. She turned off the burner. It was a relief to know Mike had kept his mouth shut about their fling but strange to discover how different his background was from hers. Until she had arrived at McGill, she had thought she was just like everyone else—ordinary, middle class—but she now realized she was lower-middle class. Her father, who had only a high school diploma, managed a hardware store, and her mom worked at a retirement home. Her mother had studied nursing but hadn't been able to pursue it because she had spent so many years out of the workforce, raising her children.

The throbbing orchestral sounds of Dead Can Dance came on, the closest Bruno ever came to being mellow, and Clara realized he had left the kitchen. She glanced into the living room and saw him flipping through his record collection. She wandered over. "Bruno, are you a member of the proletariat?"

Bruno looked up. "My grandfather was. He was a foreman at a factory in St. Henri. I was born in St. Henri, but my parents moved to the West Island. My dad's an engineer. I guess you could say we're middle class."

"I see." And Clara did. It was embarrassing to be bourgeois, but if you weren't bourgeois enough to understand distinctions, that, too, could be embarrassing.

The night before exams began, Clara sat at a computer terminal reading a feature someone had submitted to the *Daily*. Two terminals over, Mike worked on an editorial. It was nine o'clock at night, and the next issue wasn't coming out until the day after tomorrow, so they were alone in the office. Half an hour earlier, Clara had gone upstairs to fetch slices of pizza for both of them from the student bar.

The tension between her and Mike had disappeared a few weeks ago when Mike had asked Clara if she was interested in taking over the job of features editor (Una had resigned). Although Clara's schedule was full, she told Mike yes because she was flattered to be taken so seriously. He told her that other members of the *Daily* would first need to vote her in, but he doubted this would be a problem since no one else wanted the job. But getting elected hadn't turned out to be as easy as Mike had anticipated.

The agenda for the staff meeting had been full, and the meeting dragged on as various issues were discussed: an ad had to be rejected because the company had investments in South Africa, there was a shortage of exacto knives, the floor of the office was dangerously slippery because people kept forgetting to leave their boots outside on the mats. When these matters had been dispensed with, the staff considered Mike's nomination of Clara. Tim, the news editor, immediately raised objections: Clara was inexperienced, and the position of features editor was a powerful one. Benjamin complained that nobody else was running—that didn't seem democratic. Bruno stuck up for Clara, mentioning that the paper didn't publish features in every issue and that the *Daily* always had the option of running features from Canadian University Press. Tim said that maybe Clara should speak for herself, and Clara pointed out that there were no women in editorial positions. "Does that mean you want to be a token?" Tim asked. What Clara wanted was to pull out the cotton candy tufts of his blue and pink hair, but she had settled for snapping, "Obviously not." In the end, she was elected, but the vote hadn't been unanimous.

Now, as she waded through a piece on East Timor and colonialism, she was discovering the challenges of editing. Making students understand the difference between an academic essay and a feature was the biggest problem and much harder to fix than poor grammar and punctuation.

Bruno, dressed in his winter coat and boots, burst into the office. He was panting. Clara looked up from her terminal and was about to tell him that his boots were dripping grey water all over the floor when something about his expression stopped her—he looked as if he were about to cry or throw up.

"What's the matter?" she asked.

"You guys haven't heard?" Bruno's voice was strangely high and thin.

Now Mike stopped what he was doing. "Heard what?"

"Some guy just killed a bunch of women at Université de Montréal."

Clara gaped at Bruno. Mike asked, "Are you kidding?"

"I'm serious." Bruno stomped over to the boom box sitting on the counter. He turned on the radio, and the three of them listened as an announcer described a man with a gun entering a classroom at the engineering college at Université de Montréal and opening fire on the women. "I hate feminists!" he was reported to have yelled. A dozen women were now dead, and more had been rushed to the hospital.

Clara gripped the seat of her chair. She couldn't believe what she was hearing. Young women, students, just like her, dead.

When the radio report ended, Mike stood up. He ran

his hand over the top of his head. "I don't understand. Who was this guy? Was he one of their classmates?"

Bruno was lighting a cigarette and took a drag before answering. "No, he's just some nut who went crazy, like those guys in the States who go on a rampage and kill people."

Except the murders had happened here, in Montreal, a city where Clara felt comfortable walking home alone late at night. A city where people were progressive in their thinking. Part of her couldn't believe what she had just heard on the radio while another part of her felt angry and afraid.

Another report began. The police confirmed that fourteen women were dead as well as the gunman, who had committed suicide. When the killer had come into the class of sixty or so students, he had said, "I want the women." A male witness said no one had moved because everybody thought the gunman was joking. But after he took a shot at a student with a .22 calibre rifle, all the men had fled the classroom, leaving the women behind. No one had resisted or tried to stop the gunman.

An ad came on the radio, and Bruno went into the darkroom and emerged with three bottles of beer. He always kept some beer in the fridge along with the developing chemicals. She shook her head when he offered her a bottle. Mike took a beer, but, after opening it and taking a gulp, he set it down on a filing cabinet. Then he began to pace back and forth.

"We should go up there," Mike said. "Try and find a witness or something." He glanced at Bruno. "You could talk to them in French."

Bruno looked uneasy. "This happened hours ago. I'm sure everyone's left."

"Some students could be drinking in the nearest bar. You never know. We've got to go cover this. Clara, this would be a good feature for you."

Irritation crept through Clara. Mike was right—she should write about this, but what was wrong with him? How could he be so single-mindedly focused on his job? Didn't he care about what had happened to those women? "Mike, how can you even think about work right now?"

Mike's patrol of the floor halted. In a brittle tone, he replied, "Because this is important, this is newsworthy."

How dare he patronize her! Fury shot through Clara's veins. She stood up. Heard her voice climb. "It's a fucking tragedy!"

Bruno yelled, "Would you two shut up!"

Clara and Mike turned to look at Bruno, who began to bawl. While he cried noisily, Clara and Mike remained frozen. The anger pooling inside Clara made it impossible for her to comfort Bruno. She left the office and went across the hall to the washroom, where she tore off a length of toilet paper. She brought it back to Bruno. Mike was sitting at his computer terminal, although he wasn't working— he was hunched over in his seat, drinking the rest of his beer. Clara couldn't think of anything to say to either of them. She went to her computer, saved her file, shut the machine off, and then sat on the couch. Alone.

The day after the shootings, a vigil was held at the Université de Montréal for the slain women. Clara went. It was sunny out but cold. Even the mob of people spilling across the campus, mostly students from the city's universities and colleges, didn't seem to generate any heat. Clara felt her legs go numb. She was wearing a skirt with tights and army boots. The boots were new. Although she wasn't prepared to dye her hair purple or shave the sides of her head to fit in with how practically everyone else at the *Daily* looked, she had nonetheless begun dressing in the uniform of non-conformity. Her items of black clothing were worn in heavy rotation.

She looked around to see if anyone from the *Daily* was here, but, there were so many people, it was impossible to tell. She thought back to the Take Back the Night march; the rowdy cheer she had felt at that protest was excised. So, too, was her anger from last night. What she felt was quiet defeat. The cheap white candle she had brought burned quickly, the liquid wax sluicing over her fingers. She let the wax burn her skin, then harden, leaving little white crusts. The speeches, which were in French, ran past her. Everything felt so unreal, as when you stepped out into a brightly lit, noisy mall after spending two hours in the dark watching a scary movie.

At the end, as the crowd was beginning to disperse, Clara spotted Gabby Miller standing with a group of women, her hands jammed into the pockets of her navy pea jacket. Her cheeks were pink from the cold, and melting snow glistened on the dark crests of her hair. Clara watched her for a moment before slipping down the stairs and into the metro station. She wanted to talk to Gabby but didn't know what to say. She wanted to throw her arms around Gabby and be held by her, even though she barely knew the woman. It was a strange feeling for Clara to have. On the other hand, it was a strange time. Maybe she just needed a hug from somebody, somebody who wasn't male.

From the vigil, Clara headed to the *Daily*. The office was full of students standing around smoking and talking about the shootings. Clara sat on the couch listening as Bruno and Mathieu offered information that they had read or heard in the French media about Marc Lépine, the young man responsible for the deaths. Then the conversation shifted to the witnesses, to the men who had been in the classroom with the women.

Mike shook his head. "What cowards those guys were! If they had all just rushed Lépine, maybe one person would have lost his life, but everyone else would have been saved. It's not like the killer had major gun power."

Clara spoke up. "Do you think that's what you would have done?"

"Of course," Mike said as though this were the most obvious thing in the world.

Bruno crushed his cigarette butt into an ashtray and echoed Mike. "I would have."

Clara made a dismissive noise. "Right. You two would have been heroes. You wouldn't have been scared shitless. Well, guess what? Men aren't heroes."

She didn't wait to hear what they had to say. Instead, she got up from the couch and stormed out of the *Daily* office without looking at anybody. She swung the heavy, black industrial door wide open and then, turning around, she shoved her weight against the door, trying to make it slam shut. Then she went into the washroom, locked herself in a stall, and sat on a toilet seat. She closed her eyes and stuck her hands over them, under her glasses, so she was cupping her eyelids and cheeks. But it didn't help. Not being able to see couldn't keep unwanted memories from seeping into her mind.

What I did on my summer vacation, by Clara Stewart, age twelve. Me and my younger brothers went to a campground with my cousins on my dad's side of the family. It was sunny. The sun had felt nice against the soft flannel shirt she wore over her wet bathing suit. The shirt belonged to her eighteen-year-old cousin Joey, and she thought he was cute. *On the first day we all went swimming in a lake*. Joey kept running after Clara and feeling her up. It gave her a buzz between her legs, but she kept trying to get away because she didn't think it was right for him to touch her since they were cousins and wouldn't be able to get married later. *That night we had a bonfire, and the adults and older kids drank beer*. Clara also drank beer because Joey snuck some into her pop can. It tasted gross. *My younger brothers slept in one pup tent, and I slept in another*. Joey was supposed to sleep in a tent with his brothers but instead came into her tent. He was like a big, hyper dog. She thought he was going to curl up with her, but he attacked her. *I didn't really do much*. She stopped swimming, stopped eating, stopped taking walks, stopped playing with her little brothers, stopped speaking. *We left after two weeks*. It had taken her two weeks to call her mom, mostly because she didn't know how to tell her. "Kissing cousins" and "making babies" weren't the right words. (For one thing, he never kissed her.) Dirty words weren't right either. Words like "lick" and "suck" sounded like eating candy, whereas what Joey did was more like running a car over her, again and again.

Her mother made sure Clara was never left alone again with her cousin, but nothing seemed to happen to Joey. He was never arrested or beaten up. If he got into trouble at all, no one told her. Everyone just seemed embarrassed about the whole episode. Her parents told her simply to put it behind her. "Thank God, she didn't get pregnant," Clara overheard her mom tell her dad.

Clara had tried to forget. In fact, she rarely thought about the particulars of what Joey had done during those two weeks. But what she couldn't forget was that the people who were supposed to protect her didn't.

In the days following the vigil, Clara began to visit the Women's Union. She wasn't alone. Quite a few women dropped in. Women wanted to talk, women wanted to know what they could do, and Gabby Miller had ideas, suggestions. Even though exams had begun, she handed out petitions calling for greater gun control. She drafted volunteers to do phone trees to get the word out about a lecture on domestic violence scheduled at the Simone de Beauvoir Institute. She also organized a group therapy session at the Women's Union where women could talk to a counsellor about their feelings about the shootings.

Clara couldn't bring herself to go to the therapy session or the lecture, but she signed the petition. Also, instead of hanging out at the *Daily* every day, she went more often to the Women's Union. At the *Daily*, the enemy was "the oppressor," whereas at the Women's Union the enemy was "the patriarchy." At the *Daily*, everybody smoked and argued furiously; the Women's Union had a no-smoking policy, and political discussions seemed to consist of people agreeing with one another. In fact, the harshest thing that could be said of a woman was "She's not very supportive." And the feminist students did seem honestly to support one another. When two women turned up at the Women's Union with their heads shaved and announced that they had fallen in love, everyone, even the women who Clara had learned had boyfriends, said, "That's so cool." Another time that Clara stopped by, she found Gabby lying on the couch holding a tearful woman, who said to Clara, "It's okay, you can be here—I'm just remembering my abuse." Clara had fled but felt her admiration for Gabby deepen. Clara was uncomfortable with emotional displays and didn't think she would be much help in the same situation. Gabby never seemed fazed by anything.

Today, as Clara prepared for her last exam, the Women's Union was almost empty. A girl named Lisa, who was also studying for exams, sat on the couch with Clara, while Gabby did the accounts for the birth control that had been sold during the fall semester. (The Women's Union sold condoms at cost to female students.) Tracy Chapman played softly on a boom box in the background. When the song "For My Lover" came on, Gabby emerged from the back office to remark, "She's a dyke."

Lisa laughed. "You think everyone's a lesbian."

Gabby waved a hand. "Okay, so I was wrong about you. But listen to the lyrics of this song. She never says if her lover is a boy or a girl, and she talks about being chucked into a mental bin for her love, which she says can't be shaken by a man."

Although Clara didn't own any Tracy Chapman records, she had heard her songs so many times on the radio and lately in the Women's Union that she offered an opinion: "I think Tracy Chapman means *the* man, as in the system."

"She could mean both. There's no rule that says you can't be a black radical and a dyke," Gabby replied with a smile at Clara.

Lisa stood up. "I need to go home and feed my cats." After picking up her coat, mitts, and scarf, she bid Gabby and Clara goodbye, and left.

Gabby took Lisa's place on the couch. After a moment, a paper airplane looped into Clara's lap, and she looked up to see Gabby winking at her.

"That is so immature," Clara said. "That is so grade-school boy."

"Gilbert tugging on Anne's braids?"

"Exactly," said Clara, although she couldn't imagine a guy making a reference to a Lucy Maud Montgomery novel.

"Aren't you used to guys? You work at the *Daily*."

"Lately, I've been hanging out here, in case you haven't noticed."

"I have noticed, and I was wondering why." Gabby stared at Clara, who began to unfold the paper airplane, to smooth out the crinkles of paper while she thought about how to answer the question. She was disappointed with the guys at the *Daily*, but she didn't want to talk about getting mad at Mike and Bruno over what they had said about the shootings. She was sick of thinking about it.

Clara sighed. "My relationships with guys haven't been that great. It must be so much easier being a lesbian, I mean, aside from the oppression you face."

Gabby leaned forward to grin at Clara. "You know, I have been on a few dates with boys. Nice Jewish boys, who I swear read the same book on dating girls. It was always flowers on the third date, and I felt so bored I wanted to go home."

It seemed as though Gabby were trying to bond with Clara, but Clara couldn't relate to what she was saying. Dates? Clara had never dated anyone. She just slept with guys when she was horny or wanted some affection. "I wouldn't know about dating guys."

Gabby looked puzzled. "You've never had a boyfriend?"

"I didn't say that. I've just never gone on what you'd call a date. When I was sixteen, I had a boyfriend." Clara could see him in her mind. He was tall and thin and always pushing bangs out of his eyes. He had introduced her to J. D. Salinger novels and the Smiths. "He was the only guy I fell for. But it didn't work out."

"How come?"

Clara swallowed. "I wanted to have sex with him, but

— 113 —

he couldn't stay hard when we tried."

"Do you think he was gay?" Gabby asked.

This, which was an interesting idea, had never occurred to Clara, who had taken his problem much more personally. "His explanation was that I was the first girl who wanted to have sex with him that he respected, and he couldn't handle it. He thought I would take this as a compliment, but I thought it was pathetic. I guess you don't have to worry about that, being punished for wanting to have sex!"

Now Gabby sighed. "Actually, I just split up with my girlfriend because she never wanted to have sex."

This was the first time Clara had heard anything about a girlfriend. "That's too bad."

"Yeah. She's not taking the breakup well. She keeps saying things like, well, it sounds more poetic in French, but 'You're the air I breathe.'" Gabby's lower lip quivered. "I really disappointed her. I feel bad because she's a survivor, and I think she expected more from me."

"What do you mean 'survivor'?"

"Of sexual abuse."

"I see." Survivor was, Clara thought, a better word than victim. If you were a survivor, you were tough, a hero who had undergone a rite of passage. You weren't a girl putting up with ugly shit that made you feel slimed. Last summer, when she was watching *Ghost Busters* with her brothers, this thought had popped into her head about her cousin: he slimed me.

Gabby continued, "I don't think my ex is really into women. I think she's a political lesbian who'll go back to men."

"What's a political lesbian?" Clara had never heard this expression before.

"A woman who identifies as a lesbian because she doesn't

— 114 —

sleep with men. But she's not sexually into women." Gabby disdainfully rolled her eyes—she had, Clara thought, perfected that particular gesture. "Girls turn up at the Women's Union in September and seem to come out overnight as either lesbians or survivors."

Clara had an image of a field of exploding puffballs, those grey globes that in the month of September were invisible one day and splitting out of the earth the next, emitting tiny brown clouds of spores. She realized that Gabby, in an indirect way, was asking whether Clara was a survivor or a lesbian. Did one rule out the other? Did being a survivor turn you off men and make you into a fake, political lesbian who wouldn't want to have sex with her girlfriend? And why did Gabby want to know what Clara was? It wasn't any of her business.

Gabby's voice broke into Clara's thoughts. "Do you realize you keep sighing?"

Clara hadn't known she was doing this. How embarrassing. She stood up. "I should go home."

Even after Clara's parents offered her money for a plane ticket, she decided not to return to Alberta for the Christmas holidays. She lied to her parents, told them she couldn't get time off work. How could she explain that not going back was more of a gut feeling? A feeling that belonged to an angry kid: *I'm not going back there, and no one can make me.* Meanwhile, her roommates both decamped to their respective families, Bruno to the suburbs, and Mike to Florida to visit his grandparents.

Having the apartment to herself was wonderful. She was so exhausted. But her fatigue wasn't physical. She simply couldn't handle any more social interaction or new ideas.

When she had left her last exam, she had run into her professor, who had said, "Don't look so worried. You always have lots to say in class. I'm sure you did well."

"I don't know about that. I didn't manage to finish *Crime and Punishment*. I'm so busy—I have a part-time job, and I'm the features editor of the *Daily*."

Her professor's mouth puckered with distaste. "Don't tell me you're one of those student radicals."

She replied, "I would think you of all people would support social change."

Her professor laughed. "You can't seriously think your articles for the *Daily* will change the world for the better."

Clara replied huffily, "Yeah, I do." But as soon as she said this, she felt uncertain.

Nowadays, she felt uncertain about many things. She had borrowed a few lesbian novels from the McGill Women's Union and read them over the holidays. Some of the sex scenes were, well, sexy. When she had signed out the books, Gabby had winked at her and said, "Feminism is the theory, lesbianism is the practice," and Clara had blushed.

3.

On New Year's Eve, Clara waded through crusty snow to an art gallery on the Plateau holding a vernissage that Kirsten invited her to. A few days ago, Clara had taken the metro downtown to return some library books and discovered Kirsten playing guitar for spare change. She was singing a Tracy Chapman song in a register much higher than Chapman, and Clara watched as people tossed loonies, quarters, dimes, and nickels into the red beret Kirsten had left on the ground. Clara wasn't sure whether to put money in but decided to in the end. Kirsten, who had just finished singing, looked up and said, "Thanks." As she picked up a five-dollar bill from her beret, she added, "I don't speak French, but this pays my rent."

"I don't speak French either," Clara replied. "I have a retarded job selling *Gazette* newspaper subscriptions over the phone." The two of them looked at each other and smiled. Then Kirsten set her guitar in its case and began to root through a canvas knapsack that had a sticker on it that said, "I Fuck to Come, Not to Conceive." She took out several flyers and handed one to Clara, who stared at the black-and-white drawing of a woman's vagina and the words

"Pussy Power." Kirsten said, "There's an art show at this feminist gallery on New Year's Eve, and I have some photos in it. I'm not really a photographer, but I had a provocative idea."

Perhaps to create interest, Kirsten didn't say more, but she hadn't needed to, Clara thought as she turned onto a side street to the gallery. Clara's only other option for New Year's Eve was hanging out at Foufounes with her roommates, which she did all the time.

The gallery was housed in an old storefront that had probably been a depanneur. Clara walked up the cement stairs and opened a glass-paned door. There was a coat check as soon as she stepped in, and she handed over her wool coat, then entered a room with concrete floors and no furniture, just pictures on the walls and a video installation in one corner.

She looked around for Kirsten, but there was no sign of her among the women talking and smoking in little groups that seemed as tight and unyielding as military formations. A few women glanced at Clara, but, when they didn't recognize her, they returned to their cigarettes and conversation. Almost all the women seemed to have short, asymmetrical haircuts, and Clara noticed that everyone except her was wearing jeans or leggings. She was dressed in what was now her customary outfit—a black T-shirt and black cotton skirt with black army boots.

At the back of the room, drinks were being sold, and Clara decided to get one. She handed some money to a red-haired woman dispensing bottles of beer from a garbage can filled with ice. Before the redhead could grab a beer, a woman with a shaved head came up and gave her an intimate kiss. Clara tried not to stare. She had never seen two women kiss, at least not in a sexual way. Not in a movie, not even in real life at the Women's Union. It was both shocking and a little thrilling. Laurie Anderson was playing on the overhead speakers. It occurred to Clara that, not only was everyone in the room female, but the music and art were produced by women. Men didn't seem excluded so much as irrelevant.

Clara took a sip of her beer and began to wander around the gallery. The art seemed poorly done, amateurish, and it wasn't clear to her whether this was deliberate. One series of paintings caught her eye: black outlines of little girls against patterned backgrounds. The little girls were pre-pubescent, skinny with flat chests, but their mouths were adult, lips curved into a sardonic twist and covered with sexy lipstick. Clara remembered her cousin Joey giving her some makeup, which in retrospect she supposed he had stolen from his mom. Not lipstick, something else, eye-shadow maybe, as if that made her older or made up for what he was doing. She had taken the makeup, willingly, and she hated remembering that; it was worse than remembering what he had done to her.

She took a long swallow of her beer and examined the next piece of art, which turned out to be a series of Po-laroid shots thumbtacked to the wall. The images were of vaginas. Clara could see where skin had broken out; she could see blue veins on white thighs; she could see varia-tions of labia, some neat and tidy, and some puffed out, ir-regular fans of flesh. Nobody had shaved her pubic hair, but some girls had trimmed it. Some girls had shaved their legs; others hadn't. Written in marker on the white flap of each Polaroid were the words "Pussy Power." Stuck above the pictures was a paragraph of text: "The weirdest thing about being in Japan was how safe I felt. Once I walked through Tokyo at four in the morning and scared the hell out of a Japanese guy walking in front of me because I was bigger than him and a *gaijin*, a foreigner. I had to go all the way to Japan to realize how powerful I am."

Kirsten suddenly appeared, flapping a Polaroid to make it dry, and Clara realized that she had taken the pictures and written the commentary about Japan. Trailing after Kirsten was a very cute boy with hair to his shoulders—no, wait, it was a cute girl, a girl with pretty features and long hair who still managed to give the impression of being a boy. While Kirsten added her latest Polaroid to the wall, the girl stood a slight distance away, waiting for Kirsten the way boys wait for chicks to finish doing whatever they're doing.

When Kirsten noticed Clara, she said, "Hey, glad you could make it."

"Thanks for inviting me."

"If you want, we can go into the bathroom and I can take a Polaroid of your pussy and add it to the wall."

"Uh," Clara was momentarily flabbergasted. "No, that's okay."

From behind Clara, a familiar voice said, "She took mine."

Clara turned to see Gabby Miller approaching them, a beer in her hand, black jeans neatly pressed as usual, and both sleeves of her long white shirt rolled up to her elbows. It smelled as though Gabby was wearing men's aftershave.

To Kirsten, Gabby said, "This show's amazing."

"Yeah, it is," Kirsten agreed.

The woman waiting for Kirsten reached over and entangled her fingers with Kirsten's, pulling at them. Without bothering to introduce the woman, Kirsten laughed and said, "Got to go."

Gabby watched the two of them walk off. Clara had thought Gabby didn't like Kirsten, but she could now see

Gabby's feelings were more complicated. Gabby asked Clara if she liked Kirsten's pictures.

Clara decided to be honest. "I think they're a little obvious."

"In your face," Gabby said approvingly, not seeming to grasp Clara's criticism. "Do you want to know which one is mine?"

"No," Clara said automatically. No, she didn't want to see such an intimate picture of Gabby. But why not? It was feminist art. What was the big deal? The answer came to Clara, sudden and surprising, but oddly, not at all shocking. *The big deal is I'm attracted to her.* Even not knowing which picture was Gabby's vagina, Clara suddenly felt embarrassed. She glanced at the pictures again and then looked away. All those vaginas. Was that really what she wanted, to touch and lick Gabby's vagina? Clara realized Gabby was speaking to her. "Sorry, what was that?"

"I was asking if you liked the text Kirsten wrote about Japan."

Clara tried to remember what it had said. Something about scaring a Japanese guy. "Um, yeah, but I don't see how it relates to the pictures."

"I think it's about finding an unexpectedly safe space— the night, a foreign country, a relationship with a woman," Gabby replied.

"Oh." Was that the appeal of women? That they were safe? If so, why did Clara feel so nervous, so scared?

"Your beer's empty. Do you want another one?"

"No, that's okay."

"I'm going to get another one." Gabby hesitated, then said, "Don't worry—I wouldn't tell you which picture was mine. I'd be too embarrassed."

Gabby left Clara, who felt more relieved than disappointed. She watched Gabby get into line behind Kirsten and the cute woman she was with, and Clara wondered what it meant that she found these women attractive. She thought Kirsten was good-looking too, but not, she realized, in the same way, or at least it didn't mean the same thing. But did Clara find Gabby and Kirsten's date sexy because they looked like guys? *Does that mean I'm really straight?* Liking girls was scary and, yet, not liking them would be disappointing. What did she want? She had no idea. God, she wished she were thirty and had her act together.

She decided to leave the party to think. She got her coat, then looked around for Kirsten and Gabby to say goodbye. She spotted Kirsten stepping into the washroom with a woman, camera in hand, ready to photograph another vagina. Clara decided not to interrupt. Before she had a chance to look around for Gabby, she felt a hand on her arm.

"Leaving already?" Gabby asked.

"There's somewhere else I have to be," Clara lied.

"Too bad." Gabby leaned over and pressed her lips to each of Clara's cheeks. Gabby's mouth was wet and cool on Clara's skin, which was flushed from the beer. The double peck could not have been gentler, yet Clara felt it like an indent.

An hour later, shortly before midnight, Clara strode into Foufounes. She had intended to go home after the vernissage but was too full of nervous energy. She had waited in line for almost forty minutes to get into Foufounes, but the time had passed quickly: she kept rewinding and replaying the moment when Gabby had kissed her goodbye. Clara supposed she should have stayed at the gallery. What was her problem? Why was she here?

Foufounes was completely packed. She could barely move as sweaty guys in T-shirts with the sleeves hacked off squeezed by her to get more pitchers of beer. The Gruesomes were exiting the stage. They were a garage punk band whose retro sound and aesthetic appealed to Clara. The band members had bowl haircuts like the Beatles and wore black turtlenecks, as though they were existentialists hanging out in cafés in Paris. Like so many Montrealers, they seamlessly blended French, English, European, and North American culture.

"Clara."

She turned at the sound of her name and saw Mike standing in front of her, smiling. She hadn't seen Mike since he had gotten back from Florida, and his usual pallor had been replaced by a nut-brown glow.

"My God, you have a tan. That is so weird," Clara said. What was weirder than his tan, however, was how relaxed he looked.

"I tried to stay out of the sun, but I tan easily."

"Where's Bruno?"

"Chatting up a girl." Mike gestured with his chin. "Over there, by the window."

Clara craned her head and saw Bruno talking to a tiny woman with a huge skateboard. She had short blond hair and was quite cute. Clara turned back to Mike. "Looks like he's getting lucky."

"I doubt that."

"Are you always so disparaging?"

"I've got a reputation to uphold," Mike said. "Besides, Bruno dropped acid. I'm not sure he could do anything even if she wants to."

The bar erupted in noise. All around Clara, people were banging beer bottles and glasses on tables and shouting countdowns in French and English. There were popping sounds as champagne bottles were uncorked. Guys and girls kissed each other on the cheek and on the mouth. Bruno started making out with the blonde. Clara leaned forward and impulsively kissed Mike. She felt him edge his tongue into her mouth. Then he stopped and stepped back from her.

He said, "I don't think that's a good idea."

Clara ran her fingers through her hair. He was right: it was a bad idea. In fact, she couldn't understand why she had done it.

She lowered her hands. "You're right. Let's have a drink and forget that happened. But you buy. You can afford it— you're the Minister of Plenty." She said this a bit sharply.

Mike gave her a sardonic smile. "Two beers coming up."

Clara opened the door of the restaurant and saw that Gabby was already inside waiting. The restaurant was a tiny place down the street from Clara's apartment, but she thought it would be better to meet here since Gabby disliked Mike. Clara also wasn't sure she was ready to let her roommates know that she was on some kind of date with a woman. When classes started, Clara had run into Gabby at the Women's Union. Gabby suggested grabbing a bite to eat, but Clara had refused because she had to work. "Are you working tomorrow?" Gabby asked, and Clara blurted out, "Are you asking me on a date?" Gabby looked surprised but said, "Sure," as though it could be a date if that's what Clara wanted.

At the restaurant, Clara sat across from Gabby and took off her mittens, scarf, hat, and earmuffs. Earmuffs were so geeky, but the temperature had plunged. The air was dry, and it hadn't snowed in days. People were staying indoors, and there was a crystalline stillness to the city.

"I hope I'm not late."

"I'm early," Gabby said. She waved a menu at Clara. "Have you eaten here before?"

"I've had takeout. The *soupe tonkinoise* is good."

There was a small frown on Gabby's face. "I guess I thought the food would be more like Chinese."

Vietnamese had been a mistake. Clara tucked her hair behind the arm of her glasses, which were icy cold against her skin. "What *do* you like to eat?"

"Kraft Dinner mostly. I'm not much of a cook. But I eat with my mom once a week, and she makes me a decent meal. She lives by herself. My dad died of a heart attack when I was a teenager, and my older sisters are both living in Toronto. I'm the baby."

Clara said, "I'm the opposite. I have two younger brothers. They're twins, five years younger than me."

Gabby wasn't paying attention. She was distracted by the enormous aquarium across from them. The goldfish swimming around the tank were the same shiny orange as the sauce on some of the dishes. There was also a huge black fish with eyes on the side of its head that looked like a pair of hubcaps. Gabby wagged her finger at the black fish. "That thing looks so bizarre."

Before Clara could reply, the waiter arrived to take their order. Clara chose the soup and Gabby asked for spring rolls, which, when they arrived, didn't turn out to be what she had in mind (Gabby had confused egg rolls with spring rolls). As Gabby picked at her food, which was clearly unsatisfying, Clara found it impossible to enjoy her own meal. Making conversation was excruciating. In addition to their taste in food, they discovered other differences: Clara read novels while Gabby, who was a Sociology major, read theory. They didn't like the same music either. Clara found the women singers Gabby was into boring, whereas Gabby dismissed the Violent Femmes, who Clara thought were brilliant, as a "guy band." By the end of the meal, however, they did discover a mutual love of disco. Gabby had even written what sounded like a fascinating paper about anti-disco sentiment being a form of racism and homophobia. After describing the paper, Gabby said, "Do you want to go dancing? There's a women's bar not far from here."

"Sure." Clara didn't know if anything was happening between them. She always knew what to do with guys, but had no clue what two women did on a date. She was nervous. Were there rules to follow? How could she find out? God, she could use a drink.

The women's bar was below street level, so there were no windows and the walls were dark. Hanging above a tiny dance floor was an enormous disco ball spinning a rainbow of light. Some women were dancing, while others stood chatting around the bar with drinks in their hands. Most of the women were a decade or two older than Clara and Gabby. The idea of a woman her mother's age asking her to dance was frightening. But when Gabby left her by herself to get them drinks, no one even looked at Clara. She had supposed that lesbians, if not predatory, would certainly be hitting on each other, but, in fact, it seemed like getting anyone to talk to her at all would take effort. Maybe the women thought she and Gabby were a couple. Clara also noticed that the women all had short hair and wore jeans or slacks. She was wearing a black velvet dress she had found at a *friperie*. Were no women looking at her because they didn't think she could be a lesbian?

"Do I look straight?" Clara asked Gabby when she returned from the bar with drinks, a pair of gin and tonics with slices of lime.

"What do you mean?"

Clara took a gulp of her drink. "None of the lesbians I've seen so far have long hair or wear skirts or dresses."

"Do you think you're a lesbian?"

Clara had hoped Gabby would be able to answer that question. She was always saying which famous people were gay. "I don't know. Maybe I'm bi."

Gabby looked pained. "Or maybe you just don't know yet if you're a lesbian."

"What's wrong with being bi?"

Gabby shrugged. "You could be with women one minute and go back to men the next. My ex is seeing men now, and so is my ex before her. It's easier to be straight. If you can choose men, you will."

Clara thought about this. For Gabby, bisexuality was like being a liberal at the *Daily*. To be bisexual meant you weren't *committed*.

A cocktail waitress came around with a tray of shots, and Clara and Gabby gulped down two tubes each of vodka mixed with something sweet that tasted like apples. Clara was desperate to get buzzed: she wanted the leash of her thoughts and feelings to be longer and looser. Some people got angry when they drank, but she felt softer, more open.

Gabby took Clara's hand and led her to the dance floor. Gabby, it turned out, danced well. She had a loose, limber confidence and knew how to shake her hips and ass. She also knew how to match her own dancing talents to another person's rhythm and skill, or lack thereof. Clara surmised that taking women dancing was what Gabby did, that it was part of her repertoire.

After a couple of songs, Gabby stopped dancing to straighten out her underwear, which had gotten bunched up inside her jeans. As she wriggled her hips, she yelled over the music to Clara, "It's the dance of the scrunched-up boxer shorts."

"You wear boxer shorts?" Clara shouted back.

"Yeah."

Now Clara stopped dancing. "Do you want to be a man or something?"

Gabby rolled her eyes. "Do you think only men can be masculine?"

Clara considered this. "I guess not."

Gabby put her hands on Clara's hips, a sensation that was both comfortable and alarming. "How long do you want to stay here?"

"Did you want to go?" Clara asked, and Gabby nodded.

It was clear that Gabby wanted Clara to go home with her. Clara thought, I don't know if I want this; I don't know if I'll be any good at this. Why did disappointing a woman seem so much worse than disappointing a guy? God, she was also sober, despite the drinks.

"We could get a coffee," Clara suggested.

"Or just go back to my place." Gabby leaned over and lightly kissed Clara on the forehead.

The gentle kiss did nothing to reassure Clara. *What if we have sex and I discover that I'm not hot for women, that maybe I just don't like men, maybe I just don't like anything?*

Gabby lived in an apartment building downtown. The building was old and small, and the interior of Gabby's apartment was bourgeois. The rooms were large. Instead of a carpet, there were hardwood floors covered with what appeared to be Persian area rugs. Proper curtains tied with sashes hung in all the windows (Clara's bedroom curtain was a piece of cloth thumbtacked above her window). Gabby also had a real bed, not a futon or mattress, with a maroon bedspread and matching pillowcases. The only element of her bedroom not straight out of a catalogue was the row of teddy bears at the top of the bed.

"Don't you think it's mushy to have dolls?" Clara asked.

"I don't have dolls," Gabby said. "I have stuffed animals."

Clara wasn't sure what crucial distinction Gabby was making. She also didn't know whether to be embarrassed for Gabby for this gap in her sophistication or to like her for it.

Gabby moved the teddy bears to her bureau and then clambered back on the bed, patting a spot beside her for Clara.

Clara sat down. She took off her glasses and handed them to Gabby, who placed them on her night table. Then Gabby turned to Clara, and the two of them began kissing. In the lesbian-themed novels Clara had read, the moment the protagonist kissed a woman, she felt desire unlike any she had ever known, and, ta-dah, she realized she was a lesbian. But kissing Gabby wasn't like this, didn't answer any of Clara's questions about her sexual identity. Instead, it just felt like kissing, period. Kissing a girl wasn't much different from kissing a boy. If Clara had to divide the world, it would be between good and bad kissers, and Gabby was a good kisser. But Clara didn't feel aroused. Necking with Gabby was more like something she didn't mind, the way you didn't mind a cat's tongue on your hand.

Clara didn't want to be a tease (was there, she wondered, even a word for teasing another woman?), so she got on top of Gabby and pulled up her T-shirt, revealing surprisingly large breasts (the men's shirts Gabby wore covered this up). Clara slipped her hand beneath Gabby's bra to cup a breast. *I'm a girl and I'm touching another girl's breasts.* She felt as if she were getting away with something. She tended to be aware of how big her friends' breasts were, of what cup size they each wore, but she had thought she kept this knowledge for the purposes of comparison, to be reassured that she wasn't the only A-cup—maybe that hadn't been the whole story. Guys were crazy about big boobs, and she could see why. Maybe she *was* a lesbian.

She couldn't tell. She stopped touching Gabby, rolled onto her back and lay with her hands clasped over her chest like a body in a casket. Sex with boys was easy and stupid; sex with a woman was fraught and momentous.

"I know it's your first time," Gabby said, and Clara felt embarrassed that this was so obvious. Gabby continued, "It's okay, just relax."

Clara sat up. "Just relax, and you'll enjoy it. I hate when guys say that to me," she snapped.

"I'm not a guy," Gabby said in a mild tone. "If you want, we can cuddle."

Clara stared at her, but Gabby looked as if she meant it. In fact, Clara got the feeling that whatever happened tonight was up to her. This was confirmed by Gabby's next question, which was to ask Clara what she wanted.

Clara leaned back on her arms. "Tell me about your first time with a woman."

Gabby sat up. She pulled her legs to her chest, slung her arms around her knees. She suddenly seemed shy. "Well, I was seventeen and went to a gay bar where I got drunk and let a woman take me home. She turned out to be an alcoholic, and we dated for two weeks."

"That's it?" Clara said.

Gabby shrugged. "I wasn't interested in her. I was in love with a girl at school. She said she could be with either a man or a woman, but that if she went out with me, I had to promise her it would be forever. And I couldn't say that to her—I mean, I was only seventeen—so she started going out with a guy we both knew. Believe it or not, they're still together."

Clara wanted to ask Gabby how it had been to have sex with the woman at the bar. Instead she said, "Have you ever had sex with a man?"

"Yeah. Once."

"And?"

Gabby shrugged again. "Not much to say. I'm gay, and it turned out he was, too."

Clara wondered if they had had safe sex but decided not to ask that either. She knew from pamphlets at the Women's Union that lesbian sex was extremely low risk.

"Do you mind if I take off my clothes? I usually sleep in the nude," Gabby said.

Clara shook her head, and Gabby got off the bed and matter-of-factly undid her belt and slid off her jeans, bra, and boxers, leaving her clothes on the floor. Clara studied Gabby. She was curvy, except for her legs, which were rather skinny, and it seemed as though she shaved them. Clara shaved hers but hadn't expected Gabby would.

When Gabby got back into bed, Clara climbed on top of her.

"What are you doing?" Gabby asked.

Clara put her finger to Gabby's lips. "Quiet." Then Clara, without removing her clothes, did everything to Gabby she had ever wanted a guy to do to her, and she did it slowly, which was what she most wanted guys to do, and which they rarely did. Each kiss, each touch made Gabby tremble and sigh. She didn't seem to have erogenous zones—her entire body *was* one. Her skin was shockingly soft, and for the first time in Clara's life she felt like a guy, like, Lucky me! I've won this glorious prize of a girl. Gabby rubbed her breasts against Clara's chest and ground her warm, damp pussy against Clara's thigh, an area of her body she had never before considered useful in the sexual arena. But Gabby was humping Clara's thigh vigorously. I had better perform oral sex, Clara thought, recalling the lesbian novels she had read.

She wiggled downwards and began to explore. Laid a cheek against the silky fever of Gabby's thigh. Inhaled the musk of her. Licked up the slightly salty juices glazing her labia. Felt the hot pressure of muscle and bone. Clara had barely settled into a rhythm when Gabby's legs stiffened, and she cried out and clutched Clara's shoulders.

Afterwards, Gabby said, "I've never done that before."

Clara was confused. "Had a woman go down on you?"

"No, I mean come in someone's face."

That sounded so raunchy, but Clara supposed that was exactly what Gabby had so effortlessly done. "How do you usually come?"

"Rubbing or fingers."

"I see . . ." From what she read, Clara had thought the acid test of lesbianism was going down on a woman until she came. She had assumed that cunnilingus, like sexual intercourse for most guys, was the ultimate act. But maybe what was different about sex with women was that there were no set rules about who did what to whom.

Gabby rolled on top of Clara and started to kiss her breasts, but Clara stopped her. "No, I'm okay."

When Clara woke up, Gabby was staring at her. "I like watching you sleep," she said, and Clara realized Gabby liked her. Watching someone sleep was the sort of dorky thing you did when you had a crush on someone.

They wriggled closer together. They were both naked. As Clara stroked Gabby's breasts, Clara felt her cunt brim with liquid.

Gabby rolled onto her stomach and propped herself up on her elbows. "My ex told me she liked fucking her boyfriend but wanted to wake up next to her best friend. She told me this after our first time together. I think she thought I'd be a more satisfying blend, kind of like cotton underwear with enough spandex to keep it taut."

Clara looked up from where she was kissing the hairs on Gabby's forearm. "Is there a question in there?"

"Do you like sleeping with guys but want to wake up with your best friend?"

"I've never had a best friend," Clara said. "But would a best friend want to go down on me? Because that's what I'd like you to do right now."

Gabby could not stop grinning. Then she proceeded to do as Clara had asked.

Between schoolwork, the job at the *Gazette*, duties at the *Daily*, and her time with Gabby, Clara was extremely busy, yet there always seemed to be space in her head for wondering whether she was truly a lesbian. If she wasn't one, would she hurt Gabby? Their relationship was moving so quickly. Gabby wanted to spend so much time with Clara. "I don't believe in imposing artificial limits," Gabby said, teasing Clara over her insistence on spending a few nights a week by herself at her own apartment. Clara wasn't sure how comfortable she felt having sex with Gabby when Mike and Bruno could potentially overhear them, but the question of staying at Clara's place never came up. They always stayed at Gabby's apartment, but Clara didn't know whether that was because Gabby was too lazy to go to the east end, or because she didn't want to be around men, or because she lived by herself. Clara didn't protest because it was lovely to have privacy, to take hot baths without being interrupted by drunken roommates desperate to relieve their bladders after an evening of debauchery at Foufounes.

When Clara told Bruno and Mike that she was seeing Gabby Miller, they seemed less surprised by this than she was. Word got around the *Daily*, but people didn't seem bothered or at least they all did a good job of pretending. Clara also brought up lesbianism in her classes. In the fall, she had been content to write essays on the topic assigned, but now she suggested her own topics and complained when her courses didn't cover material by women, gay people, and people of colour. Every book about feminism or lesbianism that Gabby so much as footnoted in a conversation, Clara tracked down and read. For her Russian Literature class, she asked if she could write a paper on Alexandra Kollontai, a feminist Bolshevik who had promoted free love. Her professor wasn't aware that Kollontai, the world's first female ambassador, had also written novels, and Clara pounced on him, even though she had just learned this herself. The only people with whom Clara didn't discuss lesbianism were her family. She told herself that this was because she wanted to be more certain of her identity before springing the news on them.

Clara and Gabby had a lot of sex. Gabby lent Clara copies of *On Our Backs*, a lesbian porn magazine, and Clara pored over them, more curious than aroused, and learned a verb she had never heard before: fisting. Just when she had thought she could no longer be shocked, that she might be able to have sex with Gabby without feeling nervous, she was presented with new sexual milestones: S/M, dildos, and this activity with your hand that involved so much care that women in San Francisco gave workshops on how to do it. Becoming a lesbian felt like a game of Ms. Pac-Man, welcome to the next level. But even though Gabby showed Clara these magazines, she never pressured Clara sexually. Gabby didn't comment on the fact that Clara usually didn't orgasm, nor did Gabby make any suggestions about what to do in bed. In fact, Gabby would lie beneath Clara with a half-begging, half-penitent expression and say, "You decide. I like it best when you decide." (In these moments, Gabby reminded Clara of a horny Christian martyr, which, admittedly, was a strange way to think of a Jewish dyke, but there it was.) So far, what Clara liked most was teasing Gabby.

Throughout everything, Clara kept saying to herself: *I didn't know, I didn't know.* But in a way she had known—or rather—had known and hadn't known and refused to know all at the same time. When she looked back at her life wearing her new lesbian-feminist glasses, she remembered which women—and there hadn't been many, but there had been a few—whom she had found sexually attractive. There had been the twins in junior high, tall gazelles who wore their hair in long braids and were the stars of the track and field team; there had been her uncle Johnny's one-time girlfriend, Sue, who drove a bus; and also Leather Tuscadero on *Happy Days*. Females who weren't "typical" girls. Females Clara had admired while also thinking of them as girls who had flunked a test, girls who didn't grasp what it meant to be a girl. Now she saw, as she wrote in an essay, that masculinity, like high-paying jobs and space in the mosh pit, didn't belong only to men.

4.

In March, Mike announced that it was time for the criticism session at the *Daily*. Elections were coming up for next year's editorial positions, and to ensure improved working relations for the future, the editors were given the opportunity to constructively criticize one another. Clara had heard rumours about past sessions and felt a bit fearful. The process involved an editor leaving the room so that the others could critique the person. Then the editor-in-chief would go talk to the editor in private and share the comments that people had made. This reminded Clara of the sort of ritual that always ended in tears at the slumber parties of sixth-grade girls, and she doubted things would go better now. But Mike, who had never read a Judy Blume novel, wouldn't back down, so on the second weekend in March Clara found herself sitting in her own living room, reluctantly participating in the criticism session. She listened without commenting while her fellow editors discussed one another and dressed up their resentments as concerns. Bruno tried to offer balance by listing each person's positive qualities, but no one else bothered.

Soon it was Clara's turn. As she sat on her bed waiting

to hear what everyone thought about her, she wished, for the first time in her life, that she smoked. After about ten minutes, there was a knock on her door. She called out, "Come in."

Mike entered and sat down on the floor. Clara wondered if he didn't want to sit on her bed because it was a reminder of the time they had had sex.

"It wasn't that bad," Mike began.

"Yeah, right. It's Hate Week at the *Daily*, and my turn to be the rogue nation."

Mike looked up at the ceiling. "You don't spend enough time at the *Daily*. You're not committed enough."

What? That wasn't what Clara had expected. But then what had she expected? She had been afraid people would say, "We don't like you." She supposed that was a bit silly.

Mike was still speaking. "Last week, you coordinated the International Women's Day issue, and you left before the layout crew had finished."

It was true. Clara was supposed to put the paper to bed that night and had gone home an hour early to ravish Gabby. But she was also the only editor at the *Daily* with a part-time job, and she had a full course load. Mike, meanwhile, took three courses and received his cushy allowance from his parents.

"Look," Clara said. "I'm sorry about the women's issue. But, unlike you, I have a job."

"Then you'll have to decide what your priorities are. But now that you know, I'm sure you can do better next year," Mike said. His tone was kind, although he wouldn't look at her and didn't stick around to see how she was dealing with the comments. It seemed as if he wanted to get her review over with as much as she did. As he left her room, she remained sitting on her bed, gritting her teeth.

As soon as the criticism session ended, Clara left her apartment and headed to Gabby's. Gabby had said she would be at the library working late, but Clara had her own key. She walked instead of taking the metro. All week, the temperature had plunged up and down. The branches of the trees in Phillips Square were enveloped in ice, and the snow beneath her feet felt crisp. There had just been a snowstorm, and the air was filled with the sounds of spinning, squealing tires. People were struggling to free their cars from the snowbanks created when the streets had been ploughed.

When Clara opened the door to Gabby's apartment, a stranger stood in front of her, a middle-aged woman who Clara guessed had to be Gabby's mother. Although the woman was much shorter than Gabby, their features were unmistakably similar.

The woman looked startled by Clara. "You're here to see my daughter?"

"Yeah," Clara said. In a black pantsuit, black pumps, and a coating of deep red lipstick, Gabby's mother was more smartly put together than Clara had imagined. She was also better looking.

Gabby stepped forward. "Clara, this is my mom, Sharon Miller. Mom, this is my friend, Clara Stewart."

Mrs. Miller frowned at her daughter. "You give your friends the keys to your apartment?"

"She studies here sometimes. It's noisy at her place," Gabby said.

Clara was surprised by this evasion, by Gabby's refusal to acknowledge the status of their relationship. Supposedly Mrs. Miller, although she didn't approve, knew Gabby was a lesbian. Clara gave Gabby a quizzical look, but Gabby wouldn't meet her eyes.

"I'll get you that diet Coke, Mom," Gabby said. She

went into the kitchen, while Clara followed Gabby's mother into the living room. Mrs. Miller made herself comfortable in the middle of the couch, and Clara perched on the edge of an armchair.

"Clara's a pretty name," Mrs. Miller commented as she rummaged through her purse for a package of cigarettes and a lighter.

Most people remarked that it was an old-fashioned name. "Thanks," Clara said. "I was named after my grandmother."

"Here you go, Mom." Gabby set a can of pop, a glass, and a coaster on the coffee table in front of her mother. When she saw her mother's cigarettes and lighter, Gabby popped back into the kitchen and came back with an ashtray and set that down as well.

"Your doctor has told you to quit," Gabby said as she joined her mother on the couch.

Mrs. Miller didn't immediately reply. Instead, she lit her cigarette and inhaled deeply. After a few seconds, she placed the cigarette in the ashtray and coolly regarded her daughter. "It's good of you to be so concerned about me. Maybe you should be so concerned about yourself."

"Mom—" Gabby began, but her mother cut her off by raising both hands in the air.

"You know what happened to the Goldsteins last week? They were robbed. Do you want to know why, Gabby?" Mrs. Miller paused for rhetorical flourish. "Because their daughter left her purse at a nightclub. Her keys were sold within half an hour, and her parents' house was broken into and their television and stereo were carted away. All the managers of those downtown clubs deal in cocaine, you know. So, Gabby, let this be a lesson: you shouldn't give your keys away to all your friends."

"I don't," Gabby protested while looking at the floor. Her cheeks were flushed.

Clara thought that if *her* mother had been in the room, she knew exactly what Mrs. Stewart would have to say about Mrs. Miller: "Butter wouldn't melt in her mouth." Because Mrs. Miller cooked for her daughter every week Clara had imagined a warm, grandmotherly lady who was from a generation too old and frail to handle a daughter's lesbianism, but that wasn't the case here at all.

Mrs. Miller took another drag from her cigarette before continuing her conversation with her daughter. "So, on Sunday, Gabby, you'll be over for dinner?"

Gabby kept her eyes on the floor. "I already told you, yes."

Mrs. Miller said, "And you'll look after Cocoa for a few days when I go to Toronto?"

Cocoa, Clara knew, was Gabby's mother's bichon frise.

"I told you I would do that, too." Gabby stood up. "As you can see, Mom, I have company, but thanks for dropping by."

Mrs. Miller ground her cigarette into the ashtray, and Gabby leaned down and kissed her mother on the cheek. Mrs. Miller permitted rather than welcomed the kiss.

"Thanks for the food, Mom," Gabby said, and Clara noticed two bags of groceries on the kitchen table.

After her mother left, Gabby flopped onto the couch as though exhausted. "God, she's so pushy."

"Isn't it bad to say Jewish people are pushy?" Clara teased.

"Is that what you've learned at the *Daily*?" Gabby rolled her eyes. "We shouldn't insult Jews, but we should let Palestinians blow them up? Did you know there's no word in Yiddish for 'please'?"

"I don't think your mother liked me."

"Don't take it personally."

Clara swallowed. "Would it be better if you had a Jewish girlfriend?"

Gabby rolled her eyes again. "Are you kidding? That would be more tragic. Two Jewish girls throwing away their lives."

Neither of them spoke for a moment. Then Gabby remembered to ask, "How was the criticism session?"

"Not worth talking about."

Gabby made a face. "Oy. That bad?"

Clara shrugged, and Gabby reached for her. They hugged, which turned into kissing and touching. They didn't bother taking their clothes all the way off; they didn't even bother leaving the living room. Clara moved to the couch and Gabby dropped to her knees. When Clara felt the hard pressure of Gabby's mouth between her legs, all unwanted thoughts vanished. Some instinct made Clara reach down and grip Gabby's hair in her fists. Gabby's eyes widened, and Clara knew—for the first time in her life it wasn't a question—that she was going to come, that the bomb of pleasure ticking through her was ready to detonate. And she did. Sometimes, Clara realized, sleeping around was just trying to find one person you really wanted to have sex with. She had found that person.

Then it was Gabby's turn. Because she had made Clara come, Gabby was wearing a triumphant smirk on her face, and Clara decided she would wipe it away. Sticking her hand under the waistband of Gabby's boxer shorts, Clara wedged her fingers roughly into her lover. "You like it when I just do stuff to you," Clara said, almost thoughtfully, and Gabby nodded her head while looking embarrassed. They both liked when Clara was in control, but they never mentioned this. And Clara didn't want to talk about it now—she just wanted to keep touching Gabby, to watch her spark, flare, cascade.

Afterwards, they took off all their clothes and lay squished together on the couch. Gabby looked relaxed, with a dopey smile on her face, while Clara's body was a tense wire. She wanted to tell Gabby how much she cared about her, and that frightened Clara.

"Gabby, I love you." Clara had never said this to anyone before. She thought of the words as something to take out only on a special occasion—your best china that you didn't want to break or chip.

Gabby grinned as though she'd just heard great news, as though she'd just aced an exam. She said, "I love you, too, Clara." But she didn't say this the way Clara had, as if the words were being ripped out of her.

Clara stared at the bathroom mirror in shock. She had asked Bruno to cut her hair, but her new do wasn't the powerful, flamboyant statement she had hoped for. Instead, she looked as awkward as a baby bird. She had neither the beauty that made any haircut work nor the butch attitude that short hair seemed to suit. *I'm no longer pretty.*

Bruno called out, "Is it okay?"

Clara stepped out of the bathroom and watched Bruno sweep the remains of her hair into a dustpan. "No, but it's not your fault."

Bruno emptied the dustpan into the kitchen garbage. "Haven't you ever had short hair before?"

"Maybe when I was six."

"So why'd you want to cut it off?"

"I don't know," Clara lied. "I'm going to put a scarf

around it." She went into her room and took some scarves out of her closet. She picked up some hoop earrings from the top of a milk crate and put them in her ears. She had cut off her hair to show Gabby she was "committed to lesbianism."

Gabby was graduating at the end of the month and didn't know what she would be doing next year. She flung different possibilities around: she might apply to graduate school; she might stay in Montreal; she might move to Toronto or San Francisco. When Clara asked what would happen to the two of them, Gabby said, "You could come with me." But that wasn't realistic. Clara couldn't afford to go anywhere.

Maybe the uncertain future of their relationship was making them bicker. This week, they had a huge fight because Clara had gone to a Bi the Way meeting. Gabby had asked why Clara couldn't just join a coming-out group. "I'm not like you," Clara had said. "I'm just not as sure of who I am." It wasn't a question of feeling ashamed or uncomfortable; Clara felt genuinely uncertain. If she and Gabby were both lesbians, they weren't the same breed. Meanwhile, the women at Bi the Way, at least some of them, were more like Clara: they had long hair and wore skirts and lipstick; they had lots of sexual experience with men and seemed baffled and insecure about their sexuality. If they were bisexual, it was by default; it was because neither gay nor straight quite fit.

As for Clara, calling herself bi was like deciding to be an anarchist instead of a communist: you were still identifying against oppression, but you didn't have all the answers. But Gabby scoffed at Clara's fledgling bisexual politics (the politics of bisexuality being much clearer to Clara than the reality). "Bisexuals can always pass for straight," Gabby had said.

Clara, to show Gabby she didn't want to pass for straight, had cut off her hair. *But I'd rather look straight than not be pretty.*

The doorbell buzzed. It was probably Gabby. Clara tied a long, red paisley scarf around her head. The Lunachicks, an all-female band from New York, were playing tonight at Foufounes, and Clara had persuaded Gabby to go to the show with her and Bruno. She hoped Gabby and Bruno would get along.

Clara went and opened the door. Gabby stood before her, wearing a spring coat, even though it was still cold. It was early April, but winter hadn't given way to spring—there was just less winter. The existing mounds of snow had grown grey and dirty as they became infiltrated with sand, garbage, gravel, and dog shit.

Gabby kissed Clara. Then she said, "What's with the scarf?"

Clara removed the scarf, and Gabby stared at Clara's shorn head with dismay. "Why'd you cut your hair?"

Clara leaned against the door frame and began to weep.

The Lunachicks were amazing. Or rather it was amazing to watch girls play guitars so fast and so loudly. The Lunachicks were as punk as boys, as raw, silly, and aggressive. Clara could not stop staring at the drummer. For the first time in her life, she could understand why someone would want to be a groupie.

After the first set, Gabby teased Clara, "You think she's cute, eh?"

Busted. Clara flushed. "Yeah."

"It's okay. I'm not the jealous type." Gabby turned to Bruno. "You want a drink? I'm buying."

"A beer's fine but let me pay." Bruno stuffed a ten-dollar bill into Gabby's hand. She tried to give the money back but, when he wouldn't take it, she headed over to the bar.

Clara hadn't had to worry about Gabby and Bruno getting along. For all of Gabby's ideological issues with men, she managed to chat quite comfortably with both of Clara's roommates (Mike had turned up at the apartment before they left). Maybe Gabby was simply more at ease with people than Clara. The two of them didn't have much experience socializing together. So far, their relationship had existed in a bubble that didn't encompass much more than the Women's Union and Gabby's apartment.

Bruno began to sing the chorus of a Clash song. His Québécois accent disappeared entirely when he sang in English, and he could carry a tune. Clara heard him sing in the bathtub sometimes. When he stopped, Clara said, "You could be in a band, you know."

"My brother sang in a punk band," he said.

"I didn't know you had a brother." Clara had only ever heard Bruno mention his two younger sisters.

"He OD'd a few years ago."

Clara was startled. It had never occurred to her that Bruno, like Clara, had things in his life that he had folded up like a fan and tucked away. "I'm so sorry."

"Yeah, it was very punk rock of him," Bruno said dryly. He nodded his head in the direction of the Lunachicks, who were setting up again. "The singer kind of looks like my brother's old girlfriend."

Gabby reappeared with three bottles of beer. "Guess who I ran into—Kirsten. She's here with some girls she's in a band with. I didn't know she was in a band. That's so cool."

Bruno took a swallow of his beer. "Kirsten, as in used-to-go-out-with-Mike Kirsten?"

"One and the same," Clara said.

Gabby, who was about to sip her beer, stopped. "Kirsten went out with Mike?"

"Yup," Bruno said. "I'll go say hi." He left, and Gabby told Clara about a trip Kirsten was organizing to New York at the end of the month. Kirsten wanted to go to an ACT UP meeting and then start a chapter of the organization in Montreal. Gabby explained that ACT UP was a New York group that took political action to address the AIDS epidemic, but Clara already knew this: she had just run a feature from Canadian University Press about ACT UP members chaining themselves to the New York Stock Exchange to pressure a pharmaceutical company into lowering the prices of AIDS drugs. The tactic had succeeded, a rare instance of activism being more than a symbolic gesture.

"ACT UP is focused on men and male issues, but I like the idea of going to New York," Gabby concluded.

"I've never been," Clara said.

Gabby clutched Clara's arm. "Then we should go. It's an amazing city. I love its rough edges, its energy. It makes Montreal seem so pretty and delicate, Vienna meets Cincinnati."

Gabby would know: she had been to Austria. Like practically every student Clara had met at McGill, Gabby had spent a summer backpacking in Europe. Clara sighed. "I don't have the money."

"But activists will billet us, and we'll split the gas and rental cost of a van with Kirsten and her friends."

Gabby looked so excited. And Clara could use a holiday.

The day after her last exam, Clara found herself sitting in the back of a van, along with Gabby, Kirsten, and some students from Concordia University. At the border they waited for one student, who had forgotten his birth certificate, to pass through security. He had a driver's licence, but the border guards were hassling him because he looked freaky. He had bleached blond hair and reminded Clara of the replicant in *Blade Runner*, except he was shorter, skinnier, and rather fey. After about twenty minutes, the guards let him through.

After they crossed the border, the woman driving the van stopped at a McDonald's and everyone got out. The other passengers included a lesbian couple with matching crewcuts and a chubby guy named Michael who turned out to know Gabby. Their families went to the same synagogue, and they had attended some kind of Jewish children's summer camp together.

Nobody was too keen on McDonald's, but there were no better alternatives, and no one had gone to the trouble of packing sandwiches. The vegetarians in the group made do with French fries and apple pie. Afterwards, everyone sat in the van in a stupor, not saying much. People were full, and the van stank of ketchup and fried food.

Energy levels lifted when Kirsten brought out her acoustic guitar and sang songs by Tracy Chapman and the Indigo Girls. Gabby joined Kirsten on the chorus of some of the songs, while Clara felt bored. She'd rather listen to the Clash or Talking Heads. After Kirsten put her guitar away, Gabby grinned at her. "That was great."

"Yeah, I'd love to do an album," Kirsten said. "It's not very practical, but, hey, I'm in Women's Studies, which isn't going to get me a job either."

"I just finished a degree in Sociology," Gabby said. "I took a few Women's Studies courses, but McGill doesn't have a Women's Studies department."

"That's outrageous," Kirsten said. "Is there any reason to go to McGill other than to feel superior because of its so-called Ivy League reputation?"

It struck Clara that it was Kirsten who was always acting superior: she had a working-class background; she was totally out and comfortable with her bisexuality, blah, blah, blah. She was annoying, really.

"You know, Kirsten," Clara began, even though Kirsten hadn't been addressing her. "I don't know if I'd want to get a degree in Women's Studies. I'd rather start by learning about Freud and Marx and the literary canon than with critiques of them."

Kirsten tossed her head, but her brittle dreadlocks barely moved. "You want to get a degree where you learn nothing about women or queers or people of colour?"

"I didn't say that. I'd just rather get an 'A' for learning something than for writing about child abuse experiences in a journal," Clara shot back. She had heard about the looser evaluation process of some of the classes at Concordia.

"That's really offensive, Clara," Gabby snapped.

Clara was stunned. She had thought Gabby would appreciate her support. Then she felt so hurt she couldn't even look at Gabby because she knew she would start to cry. She didn't speak but didn't have to. Everyone around her began talking, desperate to fill the silence and to avoid watching a couple fight.

Clara lay in a sleeping bag on a blow-up mattress on the floor of a tiny three-room apartment in the East Village. The woman who lived in the apartment was sleeping at her girlfriend's place, and the crewcut girls in the van had taken her bedroom. Clara was in an office jammed with books and furniture. She was waiting for Gabby to return from the kitchen, where she was drinking beer with Kirsten even though it was after midnight.

It had been five o'clock when they arrived in Manhattan. By the time Kirsten figured out where they were supposed to be and parking was found, it was six-thirty and the ACT UP meeting had already begun. They trooped into a lecture hall in the Cooper Union, and, although their presence was disruptive, the people running the meeting didn't pause. While Clara and the others found seats, ACT UP members took turns talking into a microphone. Speaking rapidly, they would summarize an injustice and state what they wanted to do about it. As soon as each person finished, the moderator would point to some area of the room and say, "Anyone who wants to participate in this action should go stand over there now." Clara was amazed by how efficiently the meeting ran and how much the members accomplished. It was so different from the *Daily* or the Women's Union where everything was endlessly debated. When Kirsten suggested the Montrealers participate in a queer kiss-in planned for the next day, they trudged over to the appointed spot in the lecture hall and were given flyers with all the details.

Around twelve-thirty that night, Gabby entered the room where Clara was trying to sleep. Clara watched her strip down to her boxer shorts and put on a tank top. When Gabby saw Clara staring, she said, "You're awake."

"Yeah. Where's Kirsten?"

"Meeting some girl at a club."

Clara felt relieved. But then Gabby said, "You know, I can't imagine what you and Kirsten saw in Mike."

Clara scowled. "I wasn't in love with him or anything."

"But you had sex," Gabby said as she crawled into the sleeping bag with Clara.

"Sometimes," Clara began, "I have sex and don't know why."

"Whatever," Gabby said. "Mike sure has good taste in women."

Clara caught Gabby's reference to Kirsten and felt hurt. Although Clara wasn't certain whether she was a lesbian, she did know she was in love with Gabby. But was Gabby in love with her? Clara was beginning to wonder.

"We're here! We're queer! Get used to it!" It was five o'clock on a Friday afternoon and "here" was a demonstration. Clara, along with forty or so members of ACT UP, was lying sprawled on the steps of a corporation that had recently refused to extend its benefit plan to include same-sex partners. Most of the ACT UP members were in their twenties and dressed in jeans, Doc Martens, and leather jackets. Just about everyone, male and female, looked like gay men trying to look like skinheads. A young woman below Clara led the chanting. The toe of the woman's big black boot was pasted with a sticker of a pink triangle. Below the triangle were the words "Silence = Death." The night before, someone had given Clara a sticker with the same words, and she wasn't sure what they meant. Becoming a lesbian sometimes felt like becoming a Mason: there were so many secret codes.

The woman who had started the chanting blew a whistle, and a woman sitting beside Clara leaned over and gave her a prim kiss on the cheek. Two men on Clara's other side began groping each other's dicks, taking the concept of kiss-in to another level. People leaving the building stepped over the protesters and pretended to ignore what was going on, while people on the street gathered to watch the show. Reporters with cameras snapped pictures. A guy behind Clara lifted his shirt to show off two pierced nipples. A businessman in a suit gave them all the finger as he hurried by, and protesters shook their fists at him. Clara felt nervous, outraged, and happy all at the same time. That is, until she looked over to see a man with a video camera filming two women making out—Gabby and Kirsten.

The woman with the sticker on her boot started yelling again. "Two-four-six-eight, we don't overpopulate! Two-four-six-eight, smash the family, smash the state!"

Clara wanted to smash Kirsten's face, then Gabby's.

After the demo, Clara took off by herself. She had wanted to talk to Gabby privately, to ask what was going on between her and Kirsten, but it hadn't been possible. Gabby refused to detach herself from the group. When Clara stood a few feet apart from everyone, Gabby had manically motioned her back. Gabby wanted to go for supper at Veselka with Michael, who was her new best friend. Earlier in the day, Clara and Gabby had gone shopping for a new leather jacket with Michael. Gabby wound up purchasing a jacket for herself, which was brand new, stiff, and creaky. Clara preferred leather jackets that were worn in, but the new jacket worked for Gabby. She didn't look like a punk, though; she looked like a trendy gay boy. As she stood in front of the mirror, surveying herself in the leather jacket, Gabby said to Clara, "This is so much fun. I've never hung out with gay men before." Clara stared at Gabby as if she were a pod person. Lesbians and gay men, who only days before had been separate panels of a tent, now appeared to be zipped up to contain queerness.

Clara and Gabby were supposed to be having fun—they were on holiday in New York. Clara shouldn't be sitting alone on a bench in Tompkins Square Park, watching a homeless guy talk to pigeons. She should be visiting the Strand bookstore or looking at paintings by Andy Warhol in the Museum of Modern Art. Or even visiting the Empire State Building and Times Square, which is what Clara's family would be doing and would expect her to do. That reminded her, Clara's mother had left three messages for her this week. *I'll call back now.*

Clara walked to a payphone and discovered it was broken. Half a block away, she found one that worked and placed a collect call to her mother. Her father answered the phone but, before she even had a chance to speak to him, he put her mother on.

Her mother said, "Clara, are you all right? What are you doing in New York?"

"I'm on a trip. But I'm going back to Montreal on Sunday. I'm sorry I didn't call you sooner—I was studying for my exams. Is everything okay?"

The phone went quiet. A quiet that was hard to hear—Clara's ears were filled with the blare of the city. It was like having one speaker on your record player fuzz out.

Then her mother said, "It's your cousin Joey. He died last week in a car accident."

Clara didn't know what to say. It wasn't what she was expecting, yet she wasn't surprised.

Her mother continued, "He was under the influence, but no one else got hurt, thank God."

"Do you think he did it on purpose?" If there was one thing Clara had always understood, it was that Joey was unhappy.

"I don't know about that. Anyway, your dad's going to the funeral. It's his sister's boy after all. I just thought you should know."

"Thanks."

"Are you planning to come home this summer?"

Home. Home wasn't Alberta anymore, Clara thought. Yet Joey's death would make it easier to visit. "I'm staying in Montreal, but I could come for a visit."

"Good. Don't fuss about the money. I've done a lot of overtime lately and can send you the airfare. You give me a call when you get back from New York, okay? So I won't have to worry."

"All right." Clara hung up the phone. Joey was dead. Shit. She didn't feel happy about it and she certainly didn't feel sad. What she felt was relief. He wouldn't be able to hurt anyone else.

Some hours later—Clara had no idea how many—she made her way to an address written on a flyer in her pocket. She found herself in a non-residential area that someone she asked for directions identified as the Meatpacking District. Around her, handsome men stepped out of cabs to go to the same party where she was headed.

The party was a benefit to raise money to pay for drugs for people who had AIDS. The benefit was organized by members of ACT UP and by a new group called Queer Nation. Clara was supposed to have met Gabby and Kirsten at the apartment where they were staying, but she had stood them up. After hearing about Joey, she had drifted around. Her feelings about Joey's abuse were already thrown into the wash, had already been churned around hundreds of times. *I'm upset but it's like recycled upset.* Hunger had forced her to buy a hot dog from a vendor, but otherwise she had just walked and walked until she wound up standing in front of an industrial building, where the party she was supposed to attend with Gabby was being held.

A doorman demanded a fifteen-dollar cover charge, which surprised Clara. She had never paid a cover at a lesbian bar, and Foufounes charged only three dollars, and that was just on weekends. But she forked over the money. It was a benefit after all. Guess Clara wouldn't be drinking tonight.

Inside, the space was massive. It had probably been a factory at one time. Clara didn't know how she would find Gabby. A deejay was playing something that sounded like dance music, except there were no vocals, just a hard beat laid over blips of sound. Beams of light collided on the huge dance floor, which was full of men with their shirts off. Women had come to the party, too, although fewer of them were dancing. Also milling about were the more ambiguously gendered: boy-girls with bald heads and ripped clothes and drag queens who were more Nina Hagen than Cher. The scene was a bit like Foufounes but more sophisticated and gay.

Clara walked around but didn't see anyone she knew. When she spotted a sign for the washrooms, she decided to check them for Gabby. The lineup for the women's room was long, but there was no sign of her. Was it possible she was still waiting for Clara back at the apartment? It seemed unlikely.

Clara had to pee, so she went into the men's room, which didn't have a lineup. As she washed her hands after stepping out of a stall, a man in leather pants stared at her. She thought he was gay until she noticed his gaze was glued to her braless breasts.

"Do you have a boyfriend?" he asked.

"Yes," Clara said. She had discovered that telling strange men who hit on her that she was a lesbian didn't deter them. In fact, they came on even stronger.

"Does he beat you?"

Clara noticed that the man was wearing a collar around his neck. She realized he wasn't asking if she was abused, but, rather, if she was kinky. (The pictures in *On Our Backs* and the letters to the editor viciously denouncing them had educated Clara about S/M.)

"Only at board games," she said before fleeing.

Back upstairs, she felt someone touch her sleeve. It was Michael. "Where have you been? Gabby's been so worried about you."

A feeling of satisfaction ran through Clara, but then she saw Gabby standing a few feet away talking to Kirsten. Gamma rays of jealousy radiated through Clara as she stared at them. Kirsten was wearing a giant black T-shirt as a dress, and it barely covered her ass. She had on purple-and-black striped tights, and, on any other woman they would have looked ridiculous, the entire ensemble what the host of a children's television show might wear, but Kirsten managed to look funky and sexy. When she saw Clara staring, she turned away.

Gabby marched over to Clara, while Michael scurried off. "Where the fuck have you been?" she yelled.

The party was noisy, and Clara didn't feel like shouting back. She pointed her thumb at the stairwell and headed towards it. Gabby followed, banging her feet down the metal stairs. Together, they walked to the end of the corridor where there were hardly any people.

"Well," Gabby demanded.

Clara folded her arms across her chest. "I was walking

— *156* —

around. I didn't think it was that big of a deal. I figured you'd show up here eventually."

"What's that supposed to mean?" Gabby asked. She said this as if it were a line in a play, as if the two of them were having a fight they had planned in advance.

"You wouldn't miss a good party because of me," Clara replied. "You wouldn't want to miss the opportunity to flirt with Kirsten."

Gabby scowled. "Is that what this is about?"

"Not entirely." Clara cleared her throat. "I called my mom and I found out my cousin Joey died."

Now Gabby looked confused, as though they were driving and Clara had taken an unexpected detour. In a less annoyed tone, she said, "I've never heard you mention him. Were you close?"

Unexpectedly, Clara began to cry. "I don't know. You tell me. If you're twelve years old and your eighteen-year-old cousin that you've always looked up to because he drives dirt bikes and has a great record collection rapes you a bunch of times, does that make you close?"

Shock and disbelief rolled across Gabby's face. After a moment, she put her hand on Clara's arm. When Clara didn't move away, Gabby stepped closer and hugged Clara. Clara let her, because it felt so good, even though she knew the hug had an expiry date, that she was crying about what was happening between her and Gabby as much as she was about her cousin.

In a shaky voice, Gabby said, "I don't understand. How come I didn't know this?"

Clara sniffed and realized she had run out of tears. "I don't know. It's hard to explain. I mean, it is a big deal, and I'm almost surprised I haven't talked to you about it. At first, I didn't tell you because I was afraid you would think

I wasn't a lesbian."

Gabby released Clara. "What do you mean?"

Clara sighed. "I didn't want you to think I was a 'political' lesbian. I didn't want you to think I was with you because I'd had bad experiences with men." There was no point in adding that Clara herself had sometimes wondered if this was why she was with Gabby. "I wanted you to take me seriously."

"I do take you seriously."

"But you want to have sex with Kirsten."

"I never promised you monogamy."

Clara's toe scuffed the concrete floor. "I want you to. I want you to commit to me. And if you don't want that, I think we need to break up."

Gabby gasped. "That's not fair. I don't even know what I'm doing next year."

"That's not what I wanted to hear." Clara started to walk away, but Gabby grabbed her arm. Clara spun around. "Please. Just leave me alone."

As Clara walked into her apartment, Bruno ran down the hall towards her. "Phone. It's Gabby."

Clara groaned. "I don't want to speak to her." By the time the two of them had gotten back from New York, they had unequivocally split up. Gabby had argued with Clara: "But I still love you, I still love having sex with you." Clara had replied, "I want a commitment." Neither of them was willing to back down, and now Gabby was seeing Kirsten.

Bruno raised his hands. "Just talk to her, okay? She's phoned four times since five-thirty."

Clara usually got home from her new job as a walking messenger shortly after five, but today she had had to work late. She was exhausted. The last thing she wanted to do was process the end of her relationship. But she followed Bruno into the kitchen and picked up the phone.

"Hello."

"Clara, it's me, Gabby. Can't we have coffee?"

Clara gave Bruno a stern look. After he retreated to his room, Clara replied to Gabby, "Maybe when it's over with you and Kirsten." Another woman would have been easier for Clara to take. Even though she hadn't agreed with Gabby about bisexuality, Clara had at least thought Gabby was being sincere. Clara was almost as upset by Gabby's lack of commitment to radical lesbian feminism as she was by Gabby's unwillingness to commit to her.

Gabby wailed, "Can't we be friends? Just once I'd like to be friends with one of my exes."

Clara began wrapping the telephone cord around her forefinger. She wished she were wrapping it around Gabby's neck. "Not now."

"So you get to decide when we can be friends?"

"Yeah."

"Of course, you always have to be in control."

Clara stopped playing with the phone cord. Was Gabby trying to make her feel bad for taking charge in bed? "Wait a sec, you used to like that."

"I don't mean sex." Now Gabby sounded exasperated. "I mean, you always decided when we saw each other and how often and what kind of relationship we could have and . . . uh . . .when to tell me stuff."

Clara was silent for a moment. "You could be right, but that doesn't change anything." She sighed. "How about if we have coffee in a month?"

"Deal."

Clara hung up before Gabby could say another word.

She left the kitchen to go to her room, but, before she had time to open her bedroom door, Bruno opened his bedroom door and stared at her. Then Mike opened his door. She looked from one of them to the other; she felt as if she were being ambushed.

Mike strode up to her. He had some papers in his hand and waved them. "The new lease. Want to sign it? If you do, it means we can't kick you out. But it also means that if you want to leave, you'll be responsible for subletting your room."

"How long am I committing myself?"

"A year," Mike said.

"All right." Clara didn't mind living with Bruno and Mike. They were her friends. Bruno was holding a pen, and Clara took it from his hand and signed her new lease.

PART THREE

CROWS

Rachel picks them up in a red BMW. A flimsy rain is falling—spring on the west coast. Kelly is only a little surprised when Sonya gets into the front seat. She and Sonya haven't been getting along lately. Rachel whizzes the car through Gastown to the edge of the east end. She parks illegally: their errand won't take long. They all get out. As they walk up to the townhouse, four crows explode from a bush, a breakaway across the tarnished metal sky.

Rachel gestures towards the birds. "My granny used to say crows bring bad luck."

"Really? I've never heard that," Sonya says. "I've read they steal because they're too smart for their ecological niche."

This makes no sense to Kelly. How can a bird be too smart for its natural environment? Doesn't that mean the bird belongs in a different environment? But she doesn't say anything because she's afraid of sounding dumb. Rachel and Sonya have been to university while Kelly has not.

But then Rachel says, "Doesn't that fly in the face, so to speak, of evolutionary theory?"

Sonya shrugs. "Their brain is too big for their body.

They have evolved too fast for their role so they steal, even from one other. Like humans. We build technology that has surpassed our needs."

Kelly gets it. "Crows can't read a book or skateboard, so they steal?"

Sonya laughs. "Exactly."

Their dealer opens the door of his place with a sleepy smile. A good-looking Asian guy swinging his dreadlocks like windmills to the dancehall playing in the background. His jeans are worn low, revealing little rows of muscles on his abdomen that only endless hours at the gym can produce.

When he leaves the room to get his scales, Sonya stage-whispers, "He's so hot."

"What's with all the interest in men?" Rachel asks. "This guy, my husband. Some dyke you are."

Nearly all Kelly's girlfriends liked men or, at any rate, left her for them.

"You're married and you like girls," Sonya says.

"Yeah, and I'm not afraid to call myself bisexual," Rachel retorts.

"What turns me on about men is their top energy, not their cocks. That's also what turns me on in women, but there aren't a lot of women like that," Sonya says.

Kelly wonders if she has "top energy." She would never ask because she isn't sure she wants to hear the answer.

The dealer returns with their merchandise. Rachel takes some twenties out of her metallic tote bag and hands them over with a glance at Kelly to see if she will chip in. Kelly pretends not to notice. This morning, Rachel called, suggesting a buy. "I keep thinking about shooting up. Is that bad?" She never wanted to get high on a weeknight before; it's how she and her husband, Steven, distinguish themselves from Kelly and Sonya. But Kelly treated Rachel's question as though it were rhetorical. "We're too broke," she told Rachel, which is true. Kelly works as a letter carrier and makes a decent salary, which is swallowed by more than addiction: Vancouver is an expensive city to live in. Sonya has finagled a paltry disability cheque from the government for depression and occasionally works as a movie extra. Rachel, on the other hand, has lots of cash.

Back in the car, Rachel leads them out of downtown and across a bridge to the suburbs. They pass a billboard on the highway advertising Rachel and Steven's tanning franchise. Against a Club Med–style background, the slogan announces "Life Seem Crappy? Tan and Be Happy!" According to Steven, the secret to their success is they undercut everyone else and give discount coupons to exotic dancers. Kelly can't believe her social life revolves around these suburban yuppies. The biggest drag about being a junkie is hanging out with other junkies. No one else understands, and of course, it is preferable to hang out with junkies who have money, who sometimes buy dope for her and Sonya.

Rachel turns into a gated compound where she and Steven live in a brand new four-bedroom house with a small kidney-shaped pool and a hot tub in the back. Kelly thinks their place is tacky, but Steven runs around like Hugh Hefner living in the Playboy Mansion.

Steven meets them at the top of the stairs. He's tall and husky with blond curly hair plastered to his head. He reminds Kelly of the pin-up boys in magazines that one of her old gay roommates kept in his room. Steven grins at her and Sonya. "How's my favourite lesbian couple?"

"We're the only lesbian couple you know." Sonya's tone is light, saucy.

"You're still my favourite." Steven gives them a goofy smile, then leans over to kiss Rachel hello.

Rachel wriggles away. "So does anyone want something to eat or drink?" Even when she's strung out on smack, Rachel is the perfect hostess, emptying the ashtrays, making sure everyone has a drink and a coaster.

"I'd love a sandwich," Sonya says. "Last time we were here, you made me a cheese and cucumber sandwich."

Rachel nods and heads into the kitchen. Kelly gives Sonya a look. In a low voice, Kelly says, "If you eat, you'll just puke." Sonya sticks out her tongue at Kelly.

Steven leads Kelly and Sonya downstairs to the den, a large carpeted room with a pool table and a small bar. Rachel added a lava lamp and hanging beads across the entrance, but her attempts to infuse a funky style fail because they do not blend with the beige couch and beechwood chairs.

Sonya sits on the huge couch, tucking her bare legs beneath her like a kid, and Kelly joins her. Rachel enters carrying a tray with a sandwich on a plate and four cans of Diet Coke. As she sets the tray on the coffee table, she apologizes to Sonya for not having cucumbers.

"Don't worry about it." Sonya takes a small bite of her sandwich, then sets it down. After twirling her hair with her finger for a moment, she wanders over to the bar and pours herself a glass of gin. Sitting on the edge of the bar is the leather shaving kit where Steven keeps his gear. "Catch!" Sonya hurls the kit in Steven's direction. He seizes it with one hand, opens it, and takes out a Zippo lighter, the bottom of a pop can, cotton balls, and several syringes. Rachel brings him the bag of smack wrapped in a balloon. He shakes the dope out and places some on the bottom of the pop can. He asks Sonya to bring him some water from the bar fridge.

Kelly watches Sonya bend over the bar to reach the fridge, flashing everyone the black panties she is wearing under her short dress.

"Nice dress." Steven is shredding a cotton ball into pieces the size of Tic Tacs, but he looks up to scope Sonya's lean butt.

"Nice ass, you mean." Sonya struts back to Steven, hands him a bottle of Evian water, and sets her drink down. Then she twirls around, modelling her outfit, a tight navy-and-white dress with square-heeled black leather boots that lace up to her knees.

"Isn't that a waitress uniform?" Rachel asks.

"Yeah. I got it yesterday for six ninety-nine at Value Village. Cool, eh?"

"It's funky." Rachel's voice wavers. She never shops at thrift stores.

"You can serve me anytime." Steven winks at Sonya.

Kelly feels the muscles in her stomach pull. The game Sonya has with Steven is beginning again. They volley words back and forth with every insult layered with sex. Kelly can't wait until she is so high none of this will matter. She watches as Steven flicks his lighter on, holds it underneath the pop can bottom, and begins cooking the dope. Kelly wants to grab the stuff from him and do it herself because she knows she can do it faster. Newbie junkies, especially guys, are always into the paraphernalia. Boys and their toys.

"Kelly thinks my outfit is stupid and ugly, don't you?" Sonya pushes her breasts out.

"I never said that." Kelly presses her lips together. She had commented that Sonya spent fifty dollars of their grocery money on clothes she didn't need, in particular, the-appropriate-for-every-occasion waitress uniform.

"Is that why you're giving Kelly a hard time tonight? Because she didn't pay you enough compliments?" Rachel asks.

Sonya ignores this. She flounces onto the couch, rifles through her black rubber handbag, and digs out her rig. Kelly shifts over and helps Sonya tighten the belt around her biceps. Steven kneels in front of them with their dope, and Kelly puts the tip of Sonya's syringe into the centre of the cotton, which is puffed up like a sponge. Kelly pulls back the plunger until Sonya's share of the dope is sucked in, then places the needle flat against Sonya's skin, cranking it down the length of her vein, then expertly brings the plunger back. A tear of blood appears, and Kelly withdraws the needle. This is their ritual; Kelly helps Sonya get off, then gets off herself. Junk is what Kelly has to give Sonya. Junk makes Kelly interesting. If she weren't a junkie and a dyke, she'd be really boring, Kelly thinks. She has never been to university, has a dumb job, isn't famous—but she shoots up. And Sonya loves feeling like a sinner.

"Fix me up, will you? I hate doing it to myself." Rachel holds her syringe up to Kelly.

"No," Kelly says.

"You do it for Sonya." Rachel pouts.

"That's because I'm her girlfriend," Sonya says.

Kelly jerks her chin at Steven. "You boot her up."

Steven comes over and injects Rachel, then himself. Finally, it is Kelly's turn. When the dope is in, she leans back, feeling it flow through her veins and making her tremble the way she does when she is about to come. She goes into the zone, that sweet place in the morning when she is all silky warm under the covers, drowsy but awake enough to control her dreams. Not awake enough to feel empty and sick.

Sonya bolts for the bathroom at the very end of the den past the bar. Kelly listens to her throw up three or four times. Then she hears the gurgle of water that means Sonya is washing her mouth. Kelly forces herself to get up and propels her legs to the bathroom, feeling as if she needs a remote to command her along. She knocks on the bathroom door. "Are you okay?"

When Sonya opens the door with a toothbrush in her hand, Kelly strokes her lover's head. Sonya has this wan look, reminding Kelly of the times when Sonya isn't a brat, when she, too, is tender. The late, late nights when she holds Kelly and listens to all her secrets and stories: the girlfriend in high school who dumped her for a guy when their friends found out they were sleeping together, her mom taking off to motels when she got fed up with looking after her kids.

Sonya moves away from Kelly and opens the medicine cabinet. It's empty, except for some lipstick. "Guess they keep the good stuff upstairs," Sonya says. She takes out the tube of lipstick and unsheathes it. The colour is a dark crimson. Sonya closes the door of the medicine cabinet, leans into the mirror, and tars her lips.

Kelly loves watching women put on makeup.

Sonya rubs her lips together. She opens her mouth to speak, then closes it. She turns to Kelly, brandishing the lipstick like a marker pen. Before Kelly has time to react, Sonya grinds a red mole onto Kelly's cheek.

"You bitch." Kelly backs away from Sonya. "Why'd you do that?"

"Aw, c'mere." Sonya pockets the lipstick, then grabs the tip of a tissue from a metal dispenser on the back of the toilet. The Kleenex doesn't come out, so she pulls harder, and a clump of tissues falls out. Sonya reaches down to pick them up, then doesn't bother. Instead she sits on the floor with her legs spread and, clutching Kelly's arm, pulls her down. Then Sonya crawls on top of Kelly, who squirms, unable to get up. She is too out of it to cope with or understand her girlfriend's manic behaviour. Does Sonya want to have sex or just humiliate Kelly?

"Hi." Rachel is standing in the doorway.

"Hey, how's it going?" Sonya asks. "You know, Rachel, you should just sleep with Kelly. It's obvious you want to."

"Why? So you don't have to feel guilty about Steven?"

Sonya stands up. "No, because you're a big dyke." She rips Rachel's tiny, trendy glasses off, accidentally poking Rachel's ear with the arm of the frame. Rachel leans over, takes the glasses from Sonya, and puts them on the counter.

"She's a good screw, you know. You should fuck her," Sonya says. She bends her head so that her lips meet Rachel's.

Rachel remains still. "I think I have to throw up."

"I won't take it personally." Sonya moves aside to let Rachel into the bathroom.

Kelly scrambles up from the floor and gets out of the bathroom, allowing Rachel to slam the door shut. Kelly rubs the lipstick from her cheek with the back of her hand and hisses, "Why are you such an asshole? And why did you kiss her? She's not even your type."

"She's not. I hate her. I hate her Prada handbags, I hate the way she looks twenty when she's twenty-eight, and I hate the way she's nice to me when she doesn't even like me." Sonya prances off, and Kelly is left listening to Rachel gag. Had Rachel overheard Sonya?

Before Rachel finishes in the bathroom, Kelly follows Sonya back to the couch. Kelly sits as far away as possible from Sonya, who doesn't seem to notice. Her gaze is on Steven, as she picks up a pack of cigarettes from the coffee table, takes one out, places it between her lips. He is sprawled on the floor beside the stereo, but he immediately straightens up, takes his Zippo lighter from his pocket, and holds the flame for Sonya. She sucks on the cigarette and flicks her hair around, as if she is on a stage and Kelly and Steven are her audience. With a glance at the sound system, she says, "Steven—why don't you put on Backspin?"

Backspin is a hip hop station on satellite radio. Steven looks at the floor. "The receiver's in the car."

"Let's get it then." Sonya bends over the coffee table and crushes out her barely smoked cigarette, a prop she is done with. With the swish of a model on a catwalk, she exits the den. Steven trails her with an apologetic look at Rachel, who has just returned from the bathroom. She ignores her husband, goes to sit on the arm of the couch Kelly is now stretched out on.

Rachel says, "You know what pisses me off? I hate the way Sonya always acts so superior to me. She's the radical dyke, and I'm the straight suburban housewife. Give me a break. You pay for everything, and she's into guys." When Kelly least expects it, Rachel has the uncanny ability to nail things perfectly.

Kelly puts her arm across her eyes. "Rachel, they aren't fucking, okay? She's just torturing him. So shut up, all right?" Kelly rolls onto her side so that she faces the couch and won't have to look at Rachel.

"Get a clue. Of course they're fucking."

"Really? Then why don't you care?" Even as she says it, Kelly regrets getting involved. What is wrong with everyone? She just wants to nod out and enjoy her high. Everyone else is acting like that freaking movie Sonya once made her watch, *Who's Afraid of Virginia Woolf?* Denial is an underrated coping skill.

"It's a distraction for him. I got pregnant about a year and a half ago, and I miscarried. Steven cried for two months while I felt relieved. He's desperate for me to get pregnant again, and I don't want to touch him, let alone have kids. Do you guys want to have kids?"

When Kelly doesn't respond, Rachel taps her shoulder. Kelly rolls back over and glares at Rachel.

"Are you kidding? We can't have kids. We're junkies." Kelly's words are as taut as clothesline. The truth, which she's never admitted to anyone, even Sonya, is she would like to have kids. She sometimes wishes there were a pill she could take to become straight. She could see herself as a mom, in a station wagon with four kids, hauling them around to play hockey or whatever. Going to work and just fitting in and not having half the women refuse to go into the bathroom when she does.

Rachel hugs her legs. "I met Steven at my sister's wedding. My girlfriend had just dumped me, and my sister was getting so much attention from everyone."

Kelly closes her eyes. She hates that Sonya has gone off with Steven, but she feels her pain at a distance. Junk is a great insulator. Rachel evaporates, and Kelly enters that sterile place where the diseases others carry can't contaminate her. She remembers the first time she met Sonya. Kelly was playing pool with some guy for money when she noticed a girl with long black hair and creamy, freckled skin sitting on a bar stool sucking the pulp of a lime wedge, a cat with a fishbone. She wore a T-shirt and jeans so shredded Kelly could see more of the girl's skin than cloth. Kelly was too intimidated to do anything besides check her out. But halfway through Kelly's pool game, Sonya sailed over, seized two handfuls of Kelly's T-shirt with small, clenched fists, and said, "I want to fuck you, but I can't do it right now because I'm too high." And Sonya looked at Kelly with eyes so dark and lively they reminded her of Mexican jumping beans. Kelly fell in love. Just like that.

Rachel is shaking Kelly from her trance. "We have to call an ambulance." Rachel looks awful. White zits stick out on her chin and brown half moons shadow her eyes.

Kelly looks at the clock on the stereo and discovers it is five in the morning. Her nod seemed so short. "Why an ambulance?"

"Overdose."

Kelly pulls herself from her fog. When a shit storm begins and everyone else unravels like old sweaters, she has the power to get clear. She has been a junkie longer than any of them. Fifteen fucking years. "Who OD'd?"

"Steven."

Thank God. Kelly puts her hands on Rachel's shoulders, waits for her to calm down. Then Kelly says, "Listen to me. We'll drive him to a hospital. We won't call an ambulance. We don't want the paramedics to send cops here when they figure out what's going on. Steven'll be okay. I've OD'd twice and I'm still here. And at the hospital, you'll say you were at a party. Got it?"

Rachel nods her head like a scared doll. "They're in the bedroom."

Kelly follows Rachel upstairs, down a carpeted hall into a bedroom furnished with a king-sized sleigh bed, twin bureaus, and twin night tables. On one night table are candles, books on Buddhism and female sexuality. On the other is a single sports magazine. Lying in an inert sprawl, Steven takes up most of the bed. Sonya is perched upright on a pillow, looking out the window. She seems as far away as a distant planet, her angry presence extinguished. When she notices the two women, she glances up. "He's still breathing. I checked his pulse."

Rachel leans over Steven to stroke his cheek, but Kelly pushes Rachel out of the way and belts Steven across the face. Hitting him is necessary, but Kelly takes some grim pleasure in the act. Steven's eyes flutter open, then close again. Kelly turns to Rachel and orders her to get a wet washcloth.

Rachel scurries out of the bedroom.

Kelly slaps Steven a few more times. "C'mon, fuck face." Rachel returns with a carefully folded cloth containing two ice cubes, which Kelly rubs over his cheeks. This time, Steven stirs, but he looks like a figure in a wax museum. His fake tan is garish. He slurs when he asks what's happening to him.

"We got to get you to a hospital. You got to stand up."

Kelly grabs one of his arms while Rachel takes the other. He is very heavy. Kelly remembers someone telling her muscles weigh more than fat. As she lifts him off the bed, Kelly spots a familiar pair of black lace underwear on the floor. Something inside her shreds, is grated into small fleshy bits. She barks at Sonya, "Would you fucking get up and help us?"

"What do you want me to do?"

Kelly thinks a second. "Get him a sweater or a sweatshirt or something."

While Sonya roots around in the bedroom closet, Kelly and Rachel lead Steven through the hall and down the stairs. By the time the two of them are helping him into the back seat of the Beamer, Sonya joins them, a navy blue hoodie tucked under her arm. Both she and Rachel stand quietly, waiting for Kelly to tell them what to do.

Kelly holds out a hand. "Give me your keys, Rachel, and I'll lock up. I'll drive us to the hospital." Rachel blinks, presses her keys into Kelly's hand.

Kelly heads back inside, down to the den where she collects coats, picks up her and Sonya's gear, and puts it into Sonya's rubber handbag. The handbag is a present Kelly gave Sonya in the early days of their relationship, back when Sonya described their sex as the best of her life. But they needed to be high to fuck. That was what it took for Kelly to do what Sonya wanted her to do—slap her ass, fist her, pretend to be a rapist, whatever. Neither of them could come when they were on junk—the sex went on and on pointlessly. Sonya got bored, so they stopped fucking and now just get high. Their drug habit bonds them even more than sex. They share a sickness no one else understands. But Kelly misses sex with Sonya, and Sonya misses sex, period.

Kelly looks around the room for Steven's shaving kit. When she finds it, she unzips it and pockets what is left of his stash. In a side pouch, she discovers six one-hundred-dollar bills, which she shoves into her pocket. It is time for her and Sonya to make some new friends.

Kelly gets into the front seat of the car with Rachel, while Sonya sits in the back with Steven's legs across her lap. Beyond the windshield, an anemic sun peers around the mountains. Rachel and Steven's place does have a great view, Kelly thinks, as she guns the car out of the driveway. Rachel directs Kelly through the warren of ugly, expensive houses to the highway. As they cross the bridge into the city, Rachel undoes her seat belt so she can turn around and pat her husband's arm. "Are you sure he'll be okay?"

"What's his pulse like?"

Sonya presses her finger against his wrist for a moment.

"It's there. And he's still breathing."

"If he's breathing, he's not going to die," Kelly says. When Rachel settles back into her seat, Kelly takes one hand off the steering wheel and strokes the back of Rachel's neck to calm her down. Rachel leans into her, and Kelly realizes she could have sex with Rachel. Too bad Kelly wants only Sonya. When they arrive at the hospital, Kelly goes to the emergency room with Rachel to get the paramedics while Sonya waits with Steven. Within a few minutes, Kelly and Rachel return with two men, who lift Steven onto a stretcher.

To Rachel, Kelly says, "We're going to go home and crash." Kelly holds a pretend cell to her ear. "Call us. Let us know how he's doing." She feels bad for Rachel, but not that bad. It is time for those two amateurs to check themselves into detox. Kelly has never been to rehab. The times she's kicked, she's done it on her own.

Rachel looks as if she's about to cry. But when Sonya gives Rachel only the briefest of squeezes, Rachel's mouth hardens. "Just taking off, are you?" Rachel flaps her arms, a charade of wings.

That's what crows do, Kelly thinks. As she walks out of the parking lot, she refuses to turn around. Tagging after her is Sonya, who starts to cry. Kelly ignores this as resolutely as she ignored Rachel. But when Sonya starts hyperventilating, Kelly snatches her girlfriend by the shoulders and shakes her until she stops. "What's your fucking problem?"

Sonya's eyes dart fire. "I'm so jealous. I wanted to OD. I'm such a failure. If I died, maybe people would actually believe that there's something wrong with me, that I'm not like this on purpose."

Kelly is relieved; Sonya sounds bitter, histrionic—her

normal self. "You're not a failure. You're just a little fucked up, but who isn't? It doesn't matter."

"You want to know why I dropped out of theatre school, the real reason? It was because I overheard the coach talking about why I got a minor part in the musical. He said, 'My dear, Sonya's very good, but she'll never have the high notes.' I wasn't the best, and I thought, Fuck it, if I can't be the best, what's the point?" Sonya viciously mimics her old coach's snotty effeminacy. "'My dear, Sonya's very good, but she'll never have the high notes.'"

She continues, "Now I'm a junkie. That at least is failure on a grand scale. I prefer that to ordinary failure."

Kelly isn't into all this hand-wringing about why they're junkies. She takes Steven's money out of her pocket along with the smack, holds it all out for Sonya to see.

Sonya tosses her head back and laughs. Her white teeth are so pristine. "I love you," she tells Kelly.

"I love you, too," Kelly says.

KNIVES AND FORKS

The first thing I noticed when I entered Lou's apartment was the food laid out on a scratched harvest table. There were plump shrimp strung on skewers and redolent with garlic butter, a Caesar salad with freshly baked croutons, and crackers piled beside a wobbling pâté. Dessert was a slab of dark chocolate fanned with slivers of pears.

This was not trendy food: there were no odd pairings of sweet and savoury, no rendezvous between Far East and West Coast, no fill-in-the-blank foam. And, although Lou was a lesbian, her offerings were not politically minded: there was nothing local, organic, fair trade, or vegan on display. I *did* use local and organic ingredients when I cooked, but I found her lack of political correctness refreshing. The usual boring staples seen at lesbian potlucks—tofu chili, hummus, and tabouli—were absent. Instead, the feast before me was old-school, not exactly heart-smart, but certainly tasty.

I didn't know Lou. A friend of a friend had brought me here. But I'd seen Lou a few years before at the Lookout Bar, stalking around with a beer in her hand, her mouth in a permanent sneer. Her long hair had been dyed a ratty blue-black, and she had stuck out in a sea of the white sports shirts popular at the time. I was warned that she and her friend Karen were bad news. Once I saw her in a downtown park with a fuzzy black dog. She was lying on her back, laughing, as the dog giddily dive-bombed her, its tongue unfurling, reaching for her face. The contrast of the scene with the rebel I saw in the bar had momentarily stirred my interest, the way a slight wind picks up and drops a leaf.

When I saw Lou standing by herself in her kitchen using a tiny silver hammer to chip a bag of ice into cubes for drinks, I tapped her on the shoulder. "Great food."

"Coming from a caterer, that's high praise."

I smiled at her. "How do you know what I do?"

Lou set the hammer down. "Same way I know your name is Dana and you know mine is Lou." She grinned at my quick flush, then left the kitchen with the ice. Information flowed easily through the Ottawa lesbian community, but people didn't absorb it unless they were interested. At the end of the evening, I sought her out to say goodbye, and she said, "You're back," as if we had been talking five minutes, not two hours, earlier. When she hugged me good night, I felt a flutter of attraction.

I tended to yearn for and imagine relationships rather than be in them, so I didn't ask for her number or offer up mine. But when I saw her a month later at the Lookout Bar, I felt a mix of nausea and excitement pool in my stomach.

Lou was sitting on a bar stool chatting to Tina. I wasn't friends with Tina, but I had seen her drag king performances. She reminded me of the Fonz: she was a good-looking Italian woman who always wore a black leather jacket and always had femmes hanging off her arm. I was pretty certain she and Lou were just buddies, however. They were both butch, although Lou, with her hippie hair and high-waisted jeans, didn't seem overly concerned with her image. That suited me. I was more low femme myself, a cook with short, messy hair who lived in T-shirts, jeans, and Converse sneakers.

I felt shy but forced myself to walk over to them. Before I had a chance to say anything, Tina announced: "I have a theory about relationships." She paused to wave her cigarette in the direction of the dance floor. "Some women are spoons, and some women are forks. Spoons need to go out with spoons, and forks need to go out with forks."

I saw myself as a fork that could date only another fork. But all I said was: "Interesting theory."

"Do you think some women are knives?" Lou asked, and I could tell she liked the metaphor for herself: lean and dangerous.

I said, "A knife doesn't fit against any other piece of cutlery."

Tina laughed and clapped Lou on the shoulder. "I'm out of here," she said, leaving Lou and me to ourselves. Over the next hour, we drank and talked as well as we could over the thump of house music. Just before last call, we stumbled out of the bar. She was drunker than I was, and I put my hand on her waist to steady her. She was wearing a man's silk shirt and shuddered involuntarily at my touch. I realized she wanted me to kiss her, so I did. I pushed her up against a telephone pole, and, as we kissed, women leaving the bar gave us the thumbs-up. Then we took a cab to her place, and I passed out because of all the booze.

When I woke up in the morning, I was wearing only my underwear, and Lou was naked and grinding against me.

"What are you doing?" I asked. I was surprised by her forwardness. But I wasn't afraid: I knew I could make her stop if I wanted to.

"Don't you want to have sex?" Without waiting for an answer, she started nibbling my neck.

I raised my head and looked over her shoulder towards the window, trying to wake up. The sun glared through tightly clenched blinds into the stuffy room. It was late in the morning and early in the summer. Sweat shimmered on our bodies.

"Do you have ice cubes?"

Lou lifted her mouth from my collarbone. "Probably not," she answered too quickly.

"Don't be lazy. Go to your fridge and get me some," I commanded.

Lou got up and padded down the hall. I looked around her room for clues about her. There were piles of clothes all over the floor. A bookshelf held rows of books. I leaned over to survey them: novels old and new, serious and trashy; cookbooks; books on recovery. I flipped through a book about low self-esteem, but when I heard Lou's footsteps, I hastily put the book away.

"Here you go, girl." Lou handed me a glass filled with ice. When she got back into bed, I straddled her and lifted her arms above her head. I took an ice cube from the glass and slid it over her skin—neck, breasts, stomach. Then I slipped the ice inside her and let it melt. She winced but reached down to hold the cube in place. I moved between her legs. Her inner lips were like peeled grapes; they glistened against my mouth. I got lost in her taste and smell and couldn't decide if I was pleased or disappointed by the speed with which she came.

Lou got on top of me, kissed me, and put her hand between my legs. I was turned on, but I brushed Lou's fingers away and lay still, prickling with the desire to get up and leave. All of this was happening too quickly for me. I wanted to go away and think about her.

Lou looked down at me. "So, Dana, what do you want to do today? Want to hang out?"

"Actually, I'd like to go home."

"No problem." She paused. "Why?"

"Whenever I have sex with someone for the first time, I feel overwhelmed and have to be by myself for a while." I had never told anyone this before. Lou, thank God, did not look at me as if I were weird.

"So when do I get to see you again?"

"Tonight?" Usually I waited longer, but something told me not to this time.

"Okay." Lou rooted through a heap of clothes until she found a mashed package of cigarettes. She took a smoke out, lit it up, and joined me on the bed. She sat with her back to the wall, one leg crossed over the other. She was totally unselfconscious about being naked. She exhaled smoke slowly and stared at me, head cocked to one side. "I always thought you were snotty. I said hi to you once at Pride, and you just looked right through me."

"I probably wasn't paying attention—I wouldn't ignore someone like that. When did you decide I wasn't a snob?"

"This morning."

"You were willing to sleep with me, even though you thought I might be a jerk?"

"Why not?" She shrugged. Then, when she saw that I looked a little dismayed, she added, "I enjoyed talking to you at my party. You interested me."

"But you weren't *so* interested that you tried to get in touch with me," I teased. I really didn't mind; I liked the organic way our attraction was unfolding, but a slight flush appeared on Lou's cheeks.

"I'm bad at finishing things," she said, and the explanation seemed to dangle, itself unfinished. After a pause, she added, "I was involved with a married woman, but being her side dish didn't work out so well."

I had never been in that type of situation but said, "Isn't that how those things usually go?" It wasn't like me to tease people, to be sassy, but I felt comfortable with her. I reached over and put my hand on her bare leg. "I remember seeing you around in the bars a few years ago but not lately."

"I used to go out every night of the week. Now I'm in AA. Last night was a screw-up. That was the first drink I've had in over a year."

"I see," I said, although I didn't really.

Lou stood up to stub out her unfinished cigarette in an ashtray brimming with butts and then started to get dressed. I put on my clothes. I couldn't find one of my socks, but Lou retrieved it from under her bed.

As I put on my sock, I said, "I once saw you in a park with a dog. Did you use to have a dog?"

"Yeah, Blue. He died. He got out and was run over. Guess I left my door open." Lou indicated the front of her apartment with a sweep of her arm. "That's when I quit drinking."

"Blue, that's a cool name."

"I named him after the beer."

I liked the marbling of wryness and regret in her tone. I put my hand on the small of her back. I was about to go, but now my need to leave had dwindled away. "I'm sorry about your dog."

Lou scrutinized me. "You're sweet. I didn't expect that."

It turned out that Lou, like me, cooked for a living. She was a line cook at one of the big chains, while I ran a small catering business with a friend. You might think that the last thing either Lou or I would want to do when we weren't working was cook, but on our days off we made food for each other.

One night I watched her breasts swing as she rolled out the dough for pierogies while sauerkraut simmered on the stove. I came up behind her and began to touch her. The sex ended with her licking me while I thrust my hands into her shaggy hair. Afterwards, we ate pierogies dripping with sour cream and apple sauce. Lou had learned to make pierogies from her mother, who was Polish. I had thought Lou was short for Louise, but it was actually short for Lucyna.

Lou came across as a bar girl, a real tough cookie, and in some respects she was: she loved bands that guys loved, like Pink Floyd, and she told me stories about all the women she met in bars—including a woman who made her wear a jockstrap when they had sex. But she was also a bit of a geek: she spent a lot of time on the Web, she was a fan of *Star Trek*, and she had always brought home good grades. When I acted surprised by these things, she was dismissive. "My family was strict. I had no choice but to do well in school." She had lived at home until she was twenty-four, even though she and her mother didn't get along. Why they didn't get along I didn't know. Lou's bar stories seemed to be an established repertoire while stories of her childhood were rare. Once when I described the horror of my broke artist parents forcing me to buy my clothes at thrift shops, Lou said, "Try going to school with clothes your mother has sewn for you." I wanted to hear more, but she didn't expand on it. I gave her the complete narrative of my childhood; she gave me a summary: "It wasn't a good situation."

Her life was a recipe she wouldn't share.

But I didn't think about this too much. I was too enthralled with the sex, which was the best I had ever known. My body was as connected to her pleasure as it was to my own. Pleasing others had been like giving a back rub: it was a nice thing to do for someone you loved, or thought was cute, but it had never turned me on very much. None of my past affairs, with men or women, had the passion I felt with Lou.

Lou told me that before I came along, her relationships were purely sexual, and she had always left when they started to get serious. "It was just as well," Lou said with a roll of her shoulders. "My drinking was out of control, and I only would have brought some woman down with me."

Lou's one significant relationship had been with her friend Karen, who was now Tina's lover. After Lou and I had been going out for three months, Lou invited Karen and Tina over for dinner. On the evening they were to come over, we left the door of Lou's apartment open for the two of them to let themselves in. I was in the kitchen preparing a tapenade while Lou was outside on the balcony grilling steaks, which at my insistence were local and organic. I heard footsteps on the stairs and the clinking of beer bottles, and when I turned, Karen and Tina were standing in the kitchen. Like Lou, they were both about five years older than I was. Karen, whom I had seen in the past with Lou, was a thin, pretty blond with severely plucked eyebrows. She was holding a bag of chips. Tina was carrying a two-four of beer in her hands. Without asking, she opened the fridge and began putting the beer inside.

Lou came in from the balcony and introduced me to Karen. Then Lou and her friends chatted about the women they knew: who had found someone, who had broken up, and who was causing trouble at the bar last weekend. I suddenly remembered the steak and ran outside. The meat was just short of burned. When we sat down to eat, we all poked at it except Lou, who poured barbecue sauce on hers and didn't seem bothered. She also didn't seem to mind that Karen and Tina were drinking.

After a second helping of steak, Lou patted her stomach. "Yum," she said.

"Do you mind if I have a cigarette?" Karen asked me. She was sitting beside me, and I didn't smoke.

"Go ahead." I noticed that Karen had barely touched her plate. No one asked her why she hadn't eaten.

"So Lou tells me you're twenty-six years old and run your own business. You must be really together," Karen remarked.

She said this in a doubtful tone, as though being together were not a positive attribute.

"I'm heavily medicated," I replied. I said this as if it were a joke, but it happened to be true: I suffered from anxiety and depression.

Karen continued as if I hadn't spoken. "So did you meet Lou for the first time at her party?"

"I've seen both of you before in the bars."

Karen sucked hard on her cigarette. "Yeah, I met Lou at the Lookout. At first, I was a snob. She and her friends were always stumbling around drunk off their asses. I looked down on them, even though I was usually coked out of my head. I went to the bars by myself because I'd just broken up with my girlfriend of three years. We lived in the suburbs and didn't really socialize. She used to beat me up."

What Karen was saying was explosive, but her tone was low and flat. I looked more closely at Karen and saw something fearful and tired in her well made-up eyes. "That sucks," I said. My response felt inadequate, juvenile.

Tina got up from the table and began clearing our plates. She brought them to the sink and asked if anyone wanted a beer. Lou and I shook our heads while Karen nodded. Tina dangerously tossed Karen a bottle that Lou reached up and caught. Then Lou twisted the cap off the beer using the bottom of her T-shirt and handed the bottle to Karen.

I went down the hall to use the bathroom. The door was closed, and since Tina had left the kitchen, I thought maybe she was in the bathroom. When I felt hands behind me fondle my ass, I assumed it was Lou.

"Rotten," I said in an affectionate tone. I spun around to kiss Lou but found myself face to face with Tina. I glared at her. "What do you think you're doing?"

Tina lifted her palms up with an appeasing smile and slipped back down the hall. I opened the door to the washroom and found it empty. When I returned to the kitchen, Karen and Tina were making plans to leave. I felt relieved. Lou walked them to the door while I began washing the dishes. When Lou came back to the kitchen, she took my sudsy hands. "Leave them. Let's go out on the balcony."

The sky was the colour of ink, and the air was a cool kiss against my bare legs in shorts. Lou stood with her back against the brick wall of her apartment. She said, "Seems like something's bothering you."

"Tina grabbed my butt when I went to the bathroom."

Lou moved to the balcony railing and pumped her body up and down with her hands. "Is that all? Tina comes on to everyone when she's had too many."

"That's so humiliating. Why does Karen put up with it?"

"It doesn't mean anything and rarely goes anywhere.

Besides, Tina gets a lot of shit from Karen."

Lou turned to me and put her hands on my waist. As she leaned down to kiss me, a car driving through the back alley slowed to a crawl and the guys inside rolled their windows down to stare at us. They yelled that they had nine inches they were sure we wanted. Lou and I stayed quiet, and one of the guys spat out the window in disgust.

"Assholes!" I said when they had finally sped past.

"No kidding." Lou swallowed, her throat rippling. "You know, when my mom first found out I was a lesbian, she spat on me."

"That's awful," I said. I was appalled—but also pleased that Lou was telling me such an intimate story. My own parents, as Lou knew, didn't care if I brought home a woman, partly because they were liberal and partly because what I did didn't matter: they were too involved with the ongoing theatrical production that was their own relationship.

Lou picked up my hand and then dropped it. "Let's go inside."

She walked into her bedroom, took off her T-shirt and jean shorts, and lay on her back in her underwear not saying much. I got on top of her and held her. We looked into each other's eyes until we were practically hypnotized. I know that I fucked her, but afterwards I was never able to replay the memory. The experience was so intense, so in the moment that I could never retrieve it.

Lou spoke first. "That was the best sex I've ever had."

It was the best sex I'd ever had, too, but she was much more experienced than I was. I wondered if she was feeding me a line. "Isn't that a cliché?"

"Why, have women told you that before?" She sounded resentful.

"All the time," I replied flippantly. I slipped the dildo out of the metal ring and tossed it on the floor. Then I unbuckled the leather harness. The fantasy of fucking a woman was so hot, but the reality could sometimes disappoint because it was hard to keep the dildo inside a bucking woman. But this time I had managed, masterfully, so to speak.

"You're beautiful." Lou lifted my shirt over my head and began to touch my slender frame with her hands— hands that were muscular from working as a cook, hands that expected and received a response, hands that were soon slick with my juice.

Lou stopped what she was doing and picked up my dildo and harness. "I've never tried this before," she admitted, as she stood on her knees massaging and adjusting the cock. She looked way more suave and comfortable than I did wearing a dick. She growled, "Come here little girl, come to Daddy."

"That's really turning me on," I deadpanned.

Lou stopped fondling her dick to stare at me. When she realized I was kidding, she laughed. Then she said, "Do you know how great it is to have sex with someone who can laugh about it?"

Surprisingly, this was said in a serious tone. I didn't understand. Wasn't it normal to laugh in bed? What kind of women had she been having sex with anyway? And why was she looking at me with such sad eyes?

"Dana."

"Yeah?"

"I want to spend the rest of my life with you."

I smiled. "Okay."

"Okay?" Now Lou sounded a little doubtful.

"Yeah." I felt optimistic, confident. We were good together. I pulled her close, and she offered a hesitant smile. Then she rubbed my clit while keeping the dildo inside me, barely moving it. My thoughts melted apart, and I came in a series of jerks like a fish being reeled in from the dark, salty bottom.

Soon after having dinner with Karen and Tina, Lou and I had our first fight. Lou wanted us to be monogamous. I, assuming we were in it for the long haul, told her I wasn't sure either of us could safely say we would never stray. I added, "I prefer honesty to broken promises."

I woke up one fall morning to find her smoking a cigarette and looking at me with her grey eyes hard.

"I wonder which one of my friends you'll fuck," she sneered.

"What do you mean by that?" I blinked, not fully awake.

"You want non-monogamy, don't you?"

I only wanted her, but she didn't believe me. From then on, her insecurities began to erupt. She thought I would leave her because I liked my job and she didn't like hers; because I had a degree and she had dropped out of university; because I wasn't keen to have children and she thought she'd like to; because I had expressed interest in living in New York and she didn't want to; because I didn't like her friends. I didn't know how to reassure her; I used food, not words, to nurture. Didn't actions speak louder than words? She gave me all these reasons I would leave her—and then she left me.

A few weeks before we were to spend Christmas with my family, she stayed out all night. She was supposed to come over, and I kept texting her, upset and worried. She finally turned up at six in the morning and said we should break up. When I suggested therapy, her mouth twisted.

"There's someone else," she said. "Someone in my AA

group."

I didn't answer. Later that day, I went to her apartment and gathered the items I had lent her or left around: a springform pan, a Mediterranean cookbook, and a jar of truffles (she wouldn't eat those in bed with her new lover). Lou followed me into the kitchen.

"Guess that's it," she said.

"You fucked it up," I said. *Why did I also feel like a fuck-up?*

I missed Lou so much; I grieved and starved. Eating felt like putting food into a garbage chute. In the spring, I tried on some pants at Gap that turned out to be a size six. I was normally a size ten. I was surprised but shouldn't have been. I felt the same way when I heard that Lou and her new girl-friend got eighty-sixed from the Lookout after her girlfriend got too drunk and pulled a knife on a guy. Lou had hung out at the bar all winter while I stayed away. But one night in early spring after dreaming about Lou, I went to the Lookout and found her there. She was casual if a little distant. She asked me if I was seeing anyone.

"There's nobody new. Are you still with the woman you left me for?"

"We're not together." She glanced at me, and then looked away. "But I am dating."

In my dream of her the night before, I had been standing in front of a banquet table laden with food. I speared a gelatinous piece of translucent fish so fresh it seemed to throb. I placed it on my plate. A voice from behind me gasped, "That's blowfish." Lou was standing ahead of me in line, and I tapped her on the shoulder. "Why didn't you tell me that's fugu? That stuff can kill you."

She said, "I didn't realize you were talking to me."

It was an answer that didn't make sense. I dumped the blowfish back onto the banquet table and grabbed a piece of sushi with organic ginger and avocado. I was ravenous. My appetite had returned.

PHANTOMS

Anna picked up her crutches and pushed herself through the dining room to the living room. She really should have had her prosthesis on, but it was so uncomfortable. When she was fitted with it a few weeks ago, she had thought she would be able to put it on and walk right away. Wrong. She nearly fell over with her first step. Her stump was so slight and tender that putting weight on it hurt.

She stood in the dark looking out the window. It was ten o'clock, and Kathy wasn't home. Anna no longer bothered to ask Kathy where she went after work, where she spent most of her time on the weekends. By now, she wasn't even sure she cared.

As if on cue, a little red Neon pulled up in front of their house and stopped. Kathy got out of the passenger seat and turned to wave at the driver. The driver unrolled the window and leaned her head out. There she was, illuminated by the porch light, the woman whose presence Anna constantly felt, but whom she had never seen. She had long hair; she was pretty. Anna thought her jealousy had been amputated along with her limb, but she felt a residual twinge.

Kathy hung her coat on the coat stand, which, like the rest of their house, was Mission style—controlled serenity. When she turned on the hall light, she noticed Anna. She covered her guilt with bluster.

"Shit, Anna, you nearly gave me a heart attack. I didn't see you there!"

Anna kept her voice calm when she spoke—she knew that would upset Kathy more. "If this is your idea of being discreet, it isn't working."

Kathy fiddled with an earring. Her small gold earrings didn't match her oversized hockey shirt and jeans, but Kathy religiously wore earrings. She wasn't particularly feminine but grasped at femininity to protect herself. "I've been meaning to talk to you."

"Spare me." There was a shaky feeling in Anna's chest that came from being angry and, at the same time, being afraid of expressing her anger. "We can't afford to buy a computer-controlled leg system for me because you're such a closet case that you never asked for me to be included in your generous benefits. But you had no problem coming out at work to someone you wanted to fuck."

"I'm sorry. I know you're disappointed in me. That's nothing new." Kathy offered an apology but couldn't quite manage to hide the frustration from her tone.

Anna's voice shrilled. "I wish it had been you. I wish you had lost your leg. Bruises and whiplash—you got off cheap."

Sometimes Anna felt as if her missing leg were still there, and she would catch herself trying to take a step with it. But other times, like now, she felt as if an evil spirit had made her invisible. Invisible to Kathy. Kathy's lover was real while Anna was the poltergeist, knocking stuff over in their house.

The irritation on Kathy's face disappeared, and she came over to where Anna was standing. "I am sorry. I'm sorry about everything."

Anna exhaled. She felt stronger tonight—strong enough to admit that normal people didn't live this way. "Look, I don't want to hear it. I've had enough, and it's time we made some decisions. I want to sell our house and use the money to get a decent prosthetic limb. If there's any profit left over, we can split it. I also want the car. If you don't like those terms, well, I could sue for support, you know." Anna didn't know if that was true, but Kathy would never want to do something as public as go to court.

Kathy raised her head, and she and Anna looked at each other like cats meeting for the first time. Kathy lowered her head first. "Fine, whatever you want." Her voice was as dry and gritty as sea salt. She didn't look at Anna as she went into the hall and got her coat. She didn't turn around as their life together crumbled like five-day-old cake. She told Anna she would talk to her in the morning, and then she left.

Anna sat down on the couch, laid her crutches on the floor. She was surprised to find that she no longer felt anger or betrayal. What she felt was not very much at all. Like the time when it occurred to her to ask the doctors what they had done with her leg, and they told her it had been cremated. A woman couldn't grieve what she had already lost. Anna's breakup with Kathy had begun on the night of the accident. The accident just meant they hadn't finished what they had started.

Anna's leg had been neither lacerated nor fractured. Her knee had been dislocated severely, crushing the main artery, cutting off the blood supply to the rest of her leg and foot. As a result, her leg had to be severed.

She and Kathy had been coming home from visiting Kathy's parents, who lived in the country. A light snow fell and melted as it hit the car. Anna switched on the wipers. Kathy had had a few beers, so Anna was driving, something she didn't like to do at night. She and Kathy were arguing— their fights had become a persistent, low-grade fever— when, suddenly, Kathy asked Anna if she thought they should split up.

Anna kept her eyes on the road. Surrounding the road were fields of crisp snow glittering in the moonlight. She felt raw and cold, as if she were being rolled in the snow, even though it was warm enough in the car that the side windows were slightly fogged. "Do you?"

"You don't seem to like me anymore," Kathy whined. "And there's this woman I'm interested in, and she's interested in me."

Anna squeezed the steering wheel wishing it were her lover's throat. She had been mad at Kathy for a long time without knowing why. Having a legitimate reason felt good. "Who is she?"

"Don't worry—it's not one of our friends. I work with her, and we haven't done anything yet." Kathy checked the side-view mirror. "You should move to the right a bit. That jerk is trying to pass you."

Anna followed her gaze. A brown Subaru was tailgating them. The driver pulled out and passed her, then zoomed back into her lane. The person was driving like an idiot, but any annoyance Anna might have felt was sucked whole into the swamp of Kathy's betrayal. "Are you in love with her?"

"Anna, watch out!" In slow motion, the brown Subaru looped backwards towards her. Black ice. The driver must have hit black ice. A dark shimmer on the road—Anna could feel it, but she hadn't seen it.

In the weeks that followed the final breakup, Anna and Kathy put their house on the market. Kathy moved in with the other woman, and Anna rented a one-bedroom apartment in a high-rise. The building was hideous, and her carpets were stained. Anna realized, to her chagrin, that she missed her middle-class lifestyle more than she missed Kathy. However, her new place had an elevator, which was easier to manage with crutches, as well as a convenience store on the ground floor.

Anna wasn't mobile enough to go back to work, but she wasn't sick either. The pain she experienced was occasional, usually occurring at night: the phantom limb phenomenon. Her leg felt as if it were reattached, as if someone were twisting her foot up to her knee and around the other leg. The pain was real, although it was happening to parts of her that no longer existed. It was similar to how she felt about Kathy: what hurt, what Anna missed, was what they had once had.

Using her prosthesis was still uncomfortable. She had been told to practise by lifting up her good leg. Standing on her prosthesis with no knee, calf muscle or ankle, and using only her hip for support, she managed for a few seconds before gripping the wall. She felt herself regress to age two both physically and emotionally: she wailed. By the end of the week, however, she was able to stand for a full minute.

She tried using the prosthesis on different surfaces: cement, grass, gravel. She had to think about every move she made. A misstep could so easily result in injury. What were once ordinary—escalators, revolving doors—were now land mines.

She ran into a couple she knew: Debbie and Donna. Nurse and vet. No kids, a couple of cats, and a beagle, which Donna was walking on a long leash. The beagle tried to lick Anna, but Donna immediately reined him in.

"Stop that! Down, boy!" Donna commanded. When she managed to get the dog to sit, she glanced at Anna and then away. The guilty slide of her eyes across Anna's body wasn't sexual as it had once been.

"Sorry we haven't called," Debbie said. "We haven't talked to Kathy either. We didn't want to take sides."

"I wouldn't expect you to." As the words left her mouth, Anna realized that she was lying. She wanted someone to take her side, to say that Kathy was an asshole, that Kathy shouldn't have strayed, emotionally anyway, and that it was her fault Anna had lost her leg. Kathy had no right to talk about breaking up while Anna drove along an icy country road.

"We've been busy. It's that time of year again—the Breast Cancer Awareness March. Will you be marching—" Debbie's hand flew to her mouth.

"I don't think so," Anna replied.

"I'm really sorry." Debbie looked so stricken that Anna almost laughed.

"We should be going." Donna jerked the dog forward, and Debbie scampered after them with a weak smile.

Back in her car, Anna sat bawling until she felt a rising thickness at the back of her throat. Her friends were actually Kathy's friends, all of them bound together by playing sports, something that Anna had never enjoyed much and that was certainly not a priority for her now. Their friends were relatively attractive, successful lesbians who played golf and organized feminist fundraisers. If they had been straight men, they would have joined the Kiwanis Club and collected money for disadvantaged children. Instead, they were gay women who carefully ferreted out all the other "appropriate" gay women and dismissed the fat ones, the poor ones, and the young activists with shaved heads. Anna hadn't grasped until now how insubstantial her connection to these women was, how much she disliked them.

Anna surfed the Web for information on amputees, thinking perhaps she would join a support group. To her surprise, sex ads popped up on her screen: pictures of tiny blonde women in wheelchairs. Anna clicked on a few sites and discovered that having become what is medically termed a "transfemoral"—a word that made her think of transsexuals crossbred with wild cats, although it actually meant an above-the-knee amputee—gave her a niche market value in the sexual economy. There was a category of fetishists, typically men, who were attracted to female amputees and who called themselves "devotees." As Anna clicked through their websites and forum threads, she wondered, was their desire fucked up or subversive? A misogynist attraction to perceived helplessness or a willingness to see beyond society's narrow definition of beauty?

Hard to say. The website of a man named Andrew Bryden condemned some of his fellow devotees who had booked a hotel across the street from the National Association of Amputees Conference and made a nuisance of themselves, sexually harassing female conference participants. Andrew wrote: "We need to educate ourselves about the issues and oppression disabled women face. And, as a group, we need to come out of the closet." Anna wished Kathy had been as indignant on behalf of their relationship.

"If our relationship makes people uncomfortable," she'd say, her voice as tight and measured as the half teaspoon of sugar she permitted herself to put in her tea, "I'm not going to throw it in their faces."

Impulsively, Anna emailed Andrew. *I'm a lesbian who has recently become an amputee. You said devotees need to come out. Do you think being a devotee is similar to being gay?*

He emailed her back that night: *A month ago I was having dinner at the Del Mar with my girlfriend (well, now, ex-girlfriend), and the waitress mistook us for a mother and son. Paula is thirty-five, five years older than me. That night, she was wearing a tight black turtleneck with a short blue latex skirt, and she looked really hot. But to other people, a woman in a wheelchair cannot be sexy, cannot attract partners. Our desire for each other was invisible, which happens to lesbians (at least where I live)—you know, they're just spinster teachers who share a house to save money.*

The Del Mar. Anna and Kathy had eaten there often: an old diner in a part of town yet to be made over for a yuppie clientele. The no-smoking section was an afterthought, six booths at the back where a grey fog accumulated throughout the day from smokers' cigarettes. Kathy loved the homemade hamburgers and fries; Anna liked the neon blue sign and the kitschy 60s-style motels that ran along the strip. They made her think of adultery and private investigators working divorce cases, which, in retrospect, seemed appropriate.

Anna typed "Del Mar" in the subject line and emailed Andrew: *I live in London, Ontario. Do you?*

Close. Sarnia, he replied. Kathy's parents lived just outside Sarnia.

Anna reread his first email. Her hand went to what was left of her leg—thigh and an elastic sock that reduced swelling. She had a hard time imagining someone finding her hot. She and Kathy hadn't had sex since the accident, although, to be fair, they had been having problems in that department even before Anna had lost her leg. She typed another question: *What is it you like about amputees?*

Flawed beauty. Scars you can see.

Anna didn't know how to respond.

Another email arrived from Andrew. *I also like good-looking women wearing eye patches. What's your type?*

Anna wasn't sure she had enough experience to classify her desires. She had been with Kathy for ten years, and, before her, she'd had a few boyfriends. She replied, *I think it is more of a feeling I get from people, the way they look at me or touch me.*

A few days later at physiotherapy, Anna watched a man who was an amputee do push-ups. Anna had seen the man before, even knew a few things about him. He spoke English with a Québécois accent, had won medals in the Paralympics. He was short with a broad chest, shockingly muscular arms, and a slim, wiry leg. He was perfectly made except for his missing leg: a butterfly who had a wing pulled off by a cruel child. He was a cocktail of masculine strength and determination, difference and vulnerability—the same qualities Anna found attractive in certain lesbians. Suddenly, she understood Andrew's desire.

Kathy left messages on Anna's voice mail, mostly saying that she hoped Anna was doing okay. Anna didn't call her back. Kathy left another message saying they had received an excellent offer on their house; would Anna please call her back? Anna's line always seemed to be busy; was the phone off the hook?

Anna was online with Andrew. She messaged him before she called Kathy back: *I'll be able to afford a computer-controlled leg. A leg with sensors in the foot that will tell the knee when and how much to bend. A leg that will allow me not to "think" about walking anymore.*

Andrew replied: *I know that's good news for you. For me, women being able to hide their amputation is disappointing.*

Do you only date amputees?

Yes. But I wasn't with my ex just because she's amputated. And I won't date just any female amputee.

After their exchange ended, Anna discovered that Kathy had left her another message: "We need to meet to sign the agreement of purchase and sale. Your line is still busy."

Anna didn't want to talk to Kathy, so she pressed buttons on her phone that allowed her to deliver a voice message: "Send the documents to me by courier." Their relationship was an empty house, rooms with the doors pulled closed. Anna didn't want Kathy melting through any of the walls.

A few months after the breakup, Anna decided to go out to a bar by herself. She drove to the Robin's Nest, a lesbian bar that had managed to survive for twenty-five years. The place was located in an old agricultural society building and reminded Anna of going to the Legion with her father. The music alternated between dance and country with the odd polka number thrown in.

She was now fairly comfortable with her prosthesis, so she wore it into the bar. She wasn't sure if she could dance if someone asked her, but she doubted it would be an issue.

Most lesbians were too shy and insecure to approach a complete stranger.

Tonight proved to be the exception to the rule. A woman Anna didn't know at all immediately offered to buy her a drink, a tall, heavy butch with grey hair worn in a brush cut. Anna could barely make out what the stranger was saying above the din of the music, but she could clearly imagine what Kathy would say about the woman: "Lesbians should make an effort not to be pathetic stereotypes." Anna wasn't Kathy's first female lover, but Kathy was hers, so in the beginning Anna hadn't known enough to disagree with her.

While Anna sipped the drink, the stranger began to finger Anna's long red hair. Why wasn't Anna stopping her? Because having a woman look intimately at her without sympathy felt good. Desire rippled. Anna wanted this woman to fill her up, to fuck her with a dildo, something she had unsuccessfully begged Kathy to do. Anna wanted to be forced, to cover her memories of Kathy with bruises. A slow song came on at a lower volume, and Anna tuned into the woman's words.

"When I was about your age, I had a girlfriend with red hair just like yours. Met her in a bar in Niagara Falls. I kept trying to buy her drinks. I was so stupid I didn't get that she was a call girl. But I talked her into going out for dinner with me, and we became lovers. I thought she was the love of my life, but shit happens." A crooked smile appeared on the woman's face.

The woman wanted to have sex with Anna to feel the echo of her old life with a previous lover. But Anna was missing part of her limb, couldn't pretend for either of them to be someone else. Anna's own attraction, which suddenly vaporized, was as much a stand-in for something else as this woman's was. Anna wanted to fuck this butch to tell Kathy to fuck off.

The woman looked eagerly at Anna. "Do you want to dance?"

"No, I'm afraid I have to leave now."

When she got home, she sent Andrew an email. *Tonight a woman tried to pick me up because she has a fetish for redheads.*

A week before Anna was scheduled to get her new prosthesis, Andrew emailed to invite her to a "play party" he was organizing in his home. There would be fetishists and people into S/M, dressed up and playing with "toys."

It will be really transgressive, he wrote. In his world, "transgressive" was a high compliment.

Anna felt Kathy's judgment perch like a raptor on her shoulder. Freaks, Andrew's friends would be freaks. She IMed him: *Will a bunch of guys come onto me? Because I don't think I can handle that.*

The people I know in the scene are polite, know how to ask for permission. Besides, it will mostly be couples. But look at it this way: you won't be the only disabled person. My ex-girlfriend will be there.

What would she be like? Curiosity and something like apprehension tugged at Anna. But what she emailed Andrew was: *How will I know who you are?*

A picture arrived in her inbox. Her invisible friend became visible. He had long, wavy brown hair and the slender androgyny of Jim Morrison. He was dressed entirely in black with punkish leather wristbands. He was . . . sexy.

The following Saturday, Anna drove to Andrew's place. She was "lucky" to have lost her left rather than right leg: she could drive an automatic without too much problem. She easily found the old Victorian cottage that he owned. For wheelchair access, he had built a cement ramp leading up to the door of the house.

Anna swung gracefully up the ramp with her crutches; she was getting quite good with them. Her arms were stronger than they had ever been in her life, and her stump was light, could be moved effortlessly. She could have worn her prosthesis, but she knew it would please Andrew to see her stump, which was ever so slightly revealed beneath the hem of her short black skirt.

A nearly naked man opened the door. He was pale and skinny with stringy grey hair and glasses. He wore only a chain-mail vest, and his dick was contained in what looked like a black leather purse. Anna felt shocked. She had not been this close to a penis in over a decade. She knew she should have been prepared for this. But she wasn't.

"Hi, I'm Richard. Come in, come in. Let me take your coat and your shoe."

Richard handed her a wooden chair, and Anna sat down. He leaned her crutches against the wall and removed her shoe. Then he hung her coat in a closet and gave her back her crutches.

"I'm the houseboy for the evening, so let me know if I can be of service in any way," Richard said. "Food's up ahead."

Anna followed him down a hall and into an open-concept kitchen, dining room, and living room. It was not a large space, but the cool colours of the walls—lime, aquamarine, grey—made it seem roomier. The furnishings were a strange blend of student-style and industrial: a futon couch, record album covers tacked to the walls, various chrome items that could have been plundered from hair salons, salvage yards, and doctors' offices. A hubcap from a truck wheel served as a coffee table, and a medical exam table held an array of dishes. About half of the twenty-odd guests were standing around eating and chatting. Anna spotted some bright green pesto tortellini that looked freshly made.

"Would you like some pasta?" Richard asked. Anna nodded. He picked up a plate from the end of the buffet, spooned on pasta and Greek salad, and handed her the plate. He held up one finger, whisked off only to return seconds later with a chair. Anna sat on it, while he crouched on the floor.

"How do you know Andrew?"

"I was surfing the Web for stuff on amputees and found his site. I'm not really part of the scene. I feel like a bit of a fraud."

Richard peered over his glasses at a man licking a woman's shoes, then looked back at Anna. "I bet you think we're a bunch of sick puppies."

"I'm not judgmental," Anna lied. "How did you meet Andrew?"

"Same as you. Most of us met on the Net."

Looking around her, Anna wasn't surprised. The guests wore glasses and amulets, and despite their tight revealing latex and leather, this wasn't a crowd that went to a gym, although there was one tall, striking Goth girl swanning around. For a culture so devoted to being on the edge, fetish and S/M had an essential nerdiness. Not everyone was a geek, though: a straight couple sitting on a couch were dressed in ordinary clothes rather than vampy fetish wear. The man appeared to be in his fifties and had the straight spine and neatly tucked-in clothes of someone in the military. The woman was First Nations and had to be twenty years younger. She had short black hair and was sloppily dressed in ill-fitting big jeans and a T-shirt. She was snuggled in his lap.

Richard delivered a bottle of water to the older man. "So what are you up to now that you've retired from the force?"

Anna leaned forward in her chair so as not to miss this conversation. A police officer into S/M was somehow sinister—yet intriguing.

"I'm running a small security company. Winterizing our summer home," the man said.

"Beating my ass," his lover interrupted with a wink at Richard. Both men laughed, and the older man stroked the woman's hair.

"Something caught your eye?"

Anna turned at the sound of the voice. Andrew was looking at her with an amused expression, and she realized he had been in the room all along—he was the tall, sexy Goth chick! His long hair hung loosely down his back, and he was wearing a black vinyl dress with high boots. "You make an amazing girl." With one of her crutches, Anna pointed to a spot on the floor in front of her. "Turn around and let me see you."

"You've been watching me since you came in," Andrew replied. Nonetheless, he turned his back to her, put his hands on his hips, and tilted forward slightly. He was wearing platform heels but didn't wobble. Anna was used to women who were like men, but not men who could be women. Girly boys were the opposite of boyish girls, and yet they were the same: one gender haunting the edges of another. Anna supposed she did have a type after all.

A woman in a wheelchair rolled up to Andrew. She had the flipper arms and legs of those affected by Thalidomide, and everything about her—from her cool, long-lashed eyes to the revelation of her tiny body in a clingy dress—said, "Make no mistake, I'm hot stuff." Anna guessed she was the ex.

"Anna, this is Paula. Paula, this is my friend Anna," Andrew said.

"Nice to meet you," Anna said.

"Oh, I'm sure," Paula said. She tossed her hair over her shoulder and zipped away to another part of the room.

For that sensation of being left in the dust, Anna thought, nothing beat being on crutches while the other person was in an electric wheelchair. She was about to ask Andrew why Paula was being such a bitch when it dawned on her that Paula was jealous. Anna could have told her she didn't have any reason to be, but tonight, somehow, things were different.

At the sound of a squeal, Anna became aware that the party had started to heat up around her. While Richard bustled about putting the food away, a man painstakingly bound a woman's hands to her feet in an elaborate and intricate design. Another woman, who had a rather solemn expression, was slowly and methodically flogging a naked man. It was, Anna thought, about as sexy as watching someone chop wood. Then she noticed the First Nations woman, who now lay across her lover's lap, squirming and swearing as he spanked her. They were both fully dressed, and he used no instruments other than his bare hand, and yet what they were doing struck Anna as being more intimate and raw than anything else going on at the party.

He took his hand away. "Pull down your pants."

She shook her head, her cheeks staining red. "No, Daddy."

"What did you say?" He raised his hand above her ass.

She got up from his lap and, with her eyes on the floor, unbuttoned her jeans. She pulled her pants to her knees revealing large, plain white underwear that covered her whole butt.

Anna watched them, compelled and guilty, the way she used to look at car wrecks before she wound up in one. She knew what was going on was consensual, but it was hard to watch this woman submit sexually to an older white ex-cop without thinking about residential schools and sexual-abuse lawsuits.

Andrew kneeled in front of Anna, blocking her view. "The deal is, tonight she has to do everything he says."

"They disturb me."

"Because it turns you on," Andrew said. "I'm turning you on—does that disturb you, too?"

Anna opened her mouth to tell him no, no way, but the words stalled. When she'd fallen in love with Kathy, she'd checked the lesbian box. Her feelings for Andrew were erasing a part of herself she took pride in. Leaving her homophobic girlfriend to date a man? It was a bad cosmic joke.

Andrew leaned over the chair Anna sat on, put a hand on each of her shoulders, and kissed her. As he twisted his tongue in her mouth, desire spun through her. She remembered how humiliated she had felt by Kathy's puzzled reaction when Anna shared some of her fantasies, but she knew whispering them to Andrew would be sowing seeds in a garden. Anna felt his hand reach under her skirt. Soon she would have her permanent prosthetic limb and be able to pass unless you looked closely enough to realize that everything wasn't quite as it seemed. Like how she and Andrew would appear as a couple.

"Can I touch it?" Andrew asked.

Anna understood that he meant her stump. She nodded. She had shaved her half-leg this morning; maybe she had known all along what was materializing, what would be inevitable once they met in the flesh. Her old girlfriend was the ghost, loving Anna but hating what that made them, while Andrew was real.

His hand traced her smooth, puffed flesh. Her stump was sensitive to pain, but what she hadn't known, until now, was that it was also sensitive to pleasure. Her cunt caramelized like sugar sweating in a hot pan.

Andrew pulled away from her. "There's a limit to what we can do. I don't want to get busted for running a bawdy house."

Anna picked up her crutches. "Take me someplace where we don't have to stop."

DIFFERENT BUT EQUAL

Angie leaned through the open side window of the car to check the man whose cheek dangled from his face, his blood sluicing across the popped airbag. She dug for a pulse at his carotid.

The man was alive but might not be for much longer. His pulse was weak, and breathing dangerously shallow. She slipped an airway into his mouth, a J-shaped tube to hold the man's tongue away from his throat. Meanwhile, a firefighter crouched awkwardly in the back seat stabilized the man's neck.

"BVM," Angie yelled to Mr. Lam, a second paramedic, who'd already hooked up the Ambu bag to the oxygen and was handing it to her.

All the other paramedics called one another by their first names, but not Mr. Lam. He had been a surgeon in China, but in Canada he had to requalify and could afford only a community college paramedic program. Insisting on "mister" was a way of reminding people he should be called "doctor."

It took a few moments of coordination with the firefighter for a good c-spine position, but Angie eventually managed to help the man in the car breathe.

It had taken almost six months for Mr. Lam to trust Angie enough to let her take the lead once in a while. He was unselfconscious about asserting that men should be in charge. After they started working together, he had said to her, "You are married?" Christ, she thought irritably, haven't you been in Canada long enough to recognize a dyke? With her crewcut and large frame and every physical gesture she made a contradiction to her small hands and C-cup breasts, she continually navigated the world's double take. "Are you a man or are you a woman?" people seemed to say. "And if I can't tell, does that make you something worse?" But all she said to Mr. Lam was no, she wasn't married. "You have a hard job. A husband might not like it" was his reply. Annoyed, she decided to come out to him. "Mr. Lam, I'm a homosexual," she said. Homosexual was not a term she ever used, but it was a word he would know. His face had stiffened, and he never again referred to her personal life, although he told her plenty about his.

Angie checked the injured man's pulse. Stronger now. No need for CPR. She squeezed the BVM rhythmically, while some of the firefighters began to cut apart the car so her patient could be removed. Gary Numan had once sung about feeling safest in his car. At work, the irony of the lyrics, lost on her when she first heard the song, often struck her. Also, when she saw people pick their noses in their cars. People thought of cars as protective bubbles.

When Mr. Lam offered to take over bagging the driver, Angie gratefully stepped back and took a steadying breath before returning to the ambulance to get the spine board. That's when she saw the dog.

By the looks of it, the dog had been ejected from the car. A sleek black dog whose brains had spilled from its long head and now lay in a grey mash on the concrete. Angie felt her hands tremble and wanted to cry. She was often asked what the hardest part of being a paramedic was, and the answer was pets. People rarely bothered to buy their dog the harness and seat belt that could save it in an accident.

Accident. The word was a euphemism: the vast majority of car accidents were due to driver negligence. The word was almost as bad as the oxymoron "vehicular manslaughter." These words had the power to stop Angie's tears, to turn her grief into anger. One of the ways she dealt with a job where she had to wade through death and gather up life.

When Angie got home from her shift, it was almost midnight, and her lover, Dawn, was asleep in their bed, lying on her stomach, lovely breasts hidden beneath her, the dark twigs of her dreadlocks piled between her bare shoulders. Seeing her, Angie felt a surge of affection. They had been together for seven years, but Dawn still gave Angie a little buzz. Curled into either side of Dawn's body were their dogs, a Yorkie and a Jack Russell. Their kids, except Dawn also had a seventeen-year-old son, Ricky. Dawn had been Ricky's age when she gave birth to him, and he had been raised by Dawn and his grandmother on his father's side, a joint custody arrangement that had never been made official. At present, Ricky spent the week at his grandmother's, which was closer to his school, and the weekends with Dawn and Angie. Perhaps because Ricky already had two moms, Angie never tried to mother him. Instead, she and Ricky were somewhere between roommates and relatives. Their relationship was secure, comfortable, yet Angie had no words for it; no one seemed to. Last week, Ricky had introduced her to a new girlfriend as "Dawn's lady friend,

Miss Angie."

The words "miss" and "lady" were more fitting for Dawn than Angie. Angie thought of her relationship with her girlfriend as proof of the saying that opposites attract. Dawn's best friend had asked why, if Dawn had to be with women, she couldn't date a black woman, and Dawn had told Janeece, "I tried, but I felt like I was sleeping with my cousin." Angie understood: she, like Dawn, wanted a complement, not a copy. Angie's co-workers tended to date cops and nurses, but Dawn worked as a manicurist. Angie loved that their jobs were so different—it was a nice break. Another saying: a change is as good as a rest.

Rest. Angie knew she wouldn't get any tonight, not without chemical assistance anyway. Her thoughts were scrabbling, cornered rats. She couldn't forget the dog whose insides had become its outsides. Only after she took two sleeping pills did the image finally fuzz into darkness.

Angie felt two damp snouts push against her face as she sat up in bed. She sleepily patted each excited little dog. After a moment, they calmed down enough to sit on their haunches beside her, their ears flat, relaxed. She tried to see her alarm clock, but a silk scarf was draped over it. (Dawn loved fabrics that were soft to the touch.)

Dawn, alerted by the yapping dogs, came into the bedroom.

"What time is it?" Angie asked. She couldn't believe how exhausted she felt. Oh right, she had taken sleeping pills.

"Eleven." Dawn sat on the edge of the bed. She was wearing a yellow dress that matched her nails, which Angie noticed had been freshly done. Dawn reached over and rubbed Angie's bare leg beneath her boxer shorts. "You hungry, boo? I could make you some eggs."

Angie shook her head. Her stomach was a closed fist. She should be starving. She hadn't eaten since yesterday afternoon, and she was a big woman with a healthy appetite. But the thought of food made her nauseated. "Just coffee."

Dawn narrowed her eyes at Angie. "How was your shift yesterday?"

"Okay," Angie lied. Lying about her feelings was instinctual, yet pointless: Dawn knew her too well. In the past, Dawn wouldn't let up until they had a fight, but she'd learned to wait Angie out.

"Listen," Dawn said. "My sister told me about a house she saw that she thinks we could afford. There's an open house today. I want you to come with me."

Neither of them had ever bought a house before, but they had begun looking despite Angie's reservations. Owning a home would be great. It was, in fact, what Angie wanted most, but she didn't have enough money saved up, and Dawn's income from working part-time for a stingy Buddhist at an eco-friendly spa didn't amount to much. In addition, Dawn wanted to give Ricky the money he needed to train as a pilot, and housing prices in Halifax had skyrocketed in recent years. Even the North End, once a working-class white and black neighbourhood, was now unaffordable. But Angie knew she would probably give in to Dawn's wish for a house. Dawn's smile, when she chose the restaurant or movie, was its own reward. The only area of their relationship where Angie took complete charge was their safety. She made sure they had several types of insurance because everyone was just an accident away from being brain-damaged. She had stocked their apartment with a carbon monoxide detector, several smoke detectors, a fire extinguisher, and a roll-up fire escape ladder. And she insisted on leasing a new car, instead of buying a beater, and on getting a sensible rather than a sexy vehicle.

Outside their apartment, Angie and Dawn scanned the street looking for their Saturn.

"I can't remember where I parked the car," Angie said with a frown. This was always happening. Their car was a navy sedan, the perfect choice for an unmarked vehicle.

"Wait, I see the chimes." Dawn had recently added a decorative chain and bells to the rear-view mirror.

Angie still didn't see the car but followed Dawn, who was gliding towards the end of the street at a surprising clip given the height of her wedge heels. She must be keen to see this property, Angie thought, as she caught up to her girlfriend, who now stood beside the passenger seat waiting for Angie to unlock the door.

Dawn could drive, but Angie had never thought any of her girlfriends could drive as well as she did, so Angie always insisted on taking the wheel. Today, though, she was still groggy from the sleeping pills, so she pressed the keys into her lover's hand.

"Took some Clonazepam," Angie mumbled.

Dawn raised an eyebrow, but when Angie offered no further explanation, Dawn stepped smartly into the car. She navigated them down Quinpool Road to the Armdale Rotary.

"I'm guessing this place is off the peninsula."

"It's in Spryfield," Dawn said.

Spryfield: a strip mall; a public housing complex; a few low-rises; a trailer court; and lots of suburban housing giving way to the country, to spruce and fir trees. Nowhere decent to eat or drink and tough to manage with only one car. "I suppose it'd be quiet," Angie said after Dawn turned on to Herring Cove Road.

The one-and-half-storey house was just off the main road, down a long driveway, which would be a pain to clear in the winter. The paint on the house was peeling, and the grass was so long it enveloped the "For Sale" sign. A red "New Price" sticker had been slapped over the sign. "The good news is I think we can afford it," Dawn said as she pulled up to the house and parked beside a gleaming green SUV. She practically leapt out of the car and dashed up to the house. Angie followed more slowly, taking time to observe the missing and damaged shingles on the roof.

The screen door was unlocked, so Angie followed Dawn inside to rooms that seemed naked and bruised. There was no furniture, and there were holes all over the walls: holes from hooks and nails that had been removed, from light fixtures that had been ripped out, as well as a hole close to a baseboard where it looked as if someone had kicked in the wall. Angie glanced at Dawn, who giggled.

"What's there to laugh about?"

"This place is a dump, but I bet you anything the real estate agent will tell us it's a 'starter' home!"

Angie poked Dawn. Standing in front of them was a thin woman whose coral lips formed a frosty pucker. She wore a linen pantsuit and a lot of makeup, carefully applied. Her brown hair was pulled into a 1950s ponytail, but the prominent veins on her hands, veins a fourteen-gauge needle would easily slide into, told Angie the woman was in her forties.

Dawn's mouth dropped open. "Um, sorry."

"Do you have an appointment with me?" The agent made no effort to make her tone pleasant.

The apology evaporated from Dawn's face. "I called your office, and they said there's an open house today."

"Yes, well that's later this afternoon. Right now, I'm expecting a couple." The agent paused to assess them. "I suppose you girls can come in, though."

At least, the agent had gotten her gender right, even if at nearly forty Angie hardly qualified as a girl.

The agent briskly showed them around the downstairs. She wouldn't look at them and instead stared pointedly out windows as if she hoped Angie and Dawn would be gone when she turned around. Angie wondered why. Sometimes it was hard to figure out if they were confronting prejudice and, if so, what kind. Sometimes it wasn't so hard to tell what was going on. Last week, Angie and Dawn had been hanging out with a few friends, three white women who were talking about wild things they had done in the back of a cab. Dawn said she had never fooled around in a cab, but sometimes male cabbies would request a blow job instead of cab fare. "Uggh," she said. "Does that ever happen to any of you?" Silence filled the room; everyone was afraid of making a mistake. Angie felt annoyed, but she simply put her arm around Dawn and said, "Honey, I think you get that because you're black."

After the real estate agent led Angie and Dawn upstairs, she stood in the hallway while the two of them visited the bedrooms, which were in much better shape than the downstairs. Both rooms were large. The queen-size bed Angie and Dawn slept in with their dogs would easily fit into either room. Angie opened the door to a closet, which was also a decent size.

The agent poked her head into the room. "There's just the two bedrooms. No guest room."

The agent either assumed Angie and Dawn didn't share

the same bed or was doing her best to pretend they weren't a couple—Angie couldn't tell which.

Dawn smiled brightly at the agent. "As far as I'm concerned, that's a blessing."

The agent looked uncertain, as though she thought Dawn might be joking. "Why wouldn't you want a guest room?"

Dawn looked up from a cursory examination of her nails. "If I don't have an extra bedroom, no one in my family can try and stay with me for more than a week."

Angie laughed while the agent looked even more unsure. There was a loud buzz from the doorbell. If they bought the place, Angie thought, that bell would have to go. Oh, no! It had happened. She had caught buying fever.

"Excuse me," the agent said. "That must be the couple I'm expecting." She left them, her pumps clattering down the stairs.

Dawn wandered around the bedroom, stopping in front of the window. She lifted the sash to look outside. She had a dreamy expression on her face, and Angie could sense her arranging their furniture, landscaping the yard.

Below them, they heard the carefully modulated pitch of the agent's voice extolling the virtues of the property as she saw them. "It's an up-and-coming neighbourhood, close to schools if you have children or plan to have any."

Dawn turned from the window to face Angie. "Gee, how come we didn't get that speech?"

Angie came closer to her lover, stroked her cheek. "Honey, never mind her. You know I'd love to buy this place, but I don't think we have enough for a down payment."

"I could get another job."

Angie liked that Dawn didn't have full-time hours, that

she cooked their meals from scratch, that she never missed Ricky's wrestling matches, that the dogs were never left alone for too long. "Or I could ask my parents for some money."

Dawn sighed. "You can't count on that."

"They gave my brother and sister-in-law the down payment for their house."

"Our relationship's not the same to them."

The real estate agent's heels stabbed their way back upstairs. Behind her came the sound of more tentative feet. Dawn and Angie left the bedroom and joined the agent and a straight white couple in their mid-twenties dressed in matching khakis and Columbia parkas. The man had a short ponytail and a friendly smile; the woman had a bob and a more contained expression. She asked the agent whether the house had only one bathroom.

"Yes, just one," the agent replied. "But you could easily put another bathroom on the first floor."

"If you have the money," Dawn murmured *sotto voce* to Angie.

Angie fixed her gaze on the agent. "We're interested in the property. How much is it?"

The agent examined their faces for the first time. Then she named a price at the top of Dawn and Angie's range. "The bank owns the house and would accept less than the listed price, but with this market I think a bidding war is much more likely."

Dawn sucked in her cheeks.

The agent gave them a sympathetic nod while her eyes said, I expected as much. Aloud, she said, "It's tough for single women to get a house. Banks just don't want to take the chance."

Dawn's face tightened. "We're not single women. We're

a couple."

The agent didn't reply, but she looked as though she were having a difficult bowel movement. The man with the ponytail smothered a laugh while his girlfriend studiously stared at the floor.

After a moment, the agent turned to the man and woman. "Why don't we go downstairs so I can show you the yard?"

They nodded, and she completed the tour by leading the two of them onto the deck overlooking the backyard. Angie and Dawn followed, uninvited, but refusing to be ignored. Angie noticed a lovely ginkgo tree just beyond the deck with yellow leaves shaped like short skirts.

"Our dogs would love the yard," Dawn said.

"Do you have dogs?" Ponytail asked. He was trying to be friendly, maybe to show he wasn't homophobic or racist, or perhaps he found Dawn attractive as men often did. Dawn attributed this to having big boobs and being unavailable. Angie disagreed. One time she had told Dawn, "It's because you're sexy. Men can tell you love having sex." Dawn had protested, "You're so silly!" But she had also smiled, pleased by the description.

Ponytail continued, "We have a retriever."

"Oh yeah." Dawn's tone was just tart enough to tell him she didn't care.

Ponytail looked hurt. His girlfriend drew him aside and spoke quietly, but Angie eavesdropped while she pretended to examine possible flaws in the construction of the deck. She heard the woman say that the place was too small and needed too much work. Yes! Angie clenched her fist in victory.

"C'mon, let's go," Dawn called to Angie from inside the house. Angie went in and found the agent handing Dawn her card. They left without committing themselves.

On the way to their car, Dawn and Angie passed the agent's SUV, which she noticed had a licence plate that said "TRADE UP." There was also a fish symbol on the bumper. Angie rapped her knuckles on the hood. "Figures the bitch drives an SUV." Then she lifted her leg and mimed kicking in the tail lights of the car. "Born-again homo-phobe. That explains the attitude."

Dawn grabbed Angie's arm. "It's not worth it."

Angie was tired of things being a hassle for them. Her parents could afford to give her the extra money she needed to buy a house for her, Dawn, and Ricky. But Dawn was right: her parents would probably say no. Like likes like, there was no way to get around it. But damn, Angie wanted a house! Hot tears began to slide down her cheeks and she angrily brushed them away.

"Baby girl." Dawn threw her arms around Angie and squeezed her tightly for a moment. "It's okay to cry, you know."

But Angie always fought the urge to cry. Cry now, then you'll never stop. She was proud of her ability to stay in control. Anything could happen in this world, so the trick was to learn to handle anything. Wide awake now, she got into the driver's seat of the car. They drove away from the neighbourhood they might or might not move into. Head-ing into traffic, Angie stabbed the radio button on, but, an-noyed by the advertising, she shut the thing off.

Dawn reached over and rubbed Angie's neck, then stroked her ear. "The spa is thinking of hiring someone to do acupuncture. You know, they put those needles in your ear. It's because the ear is like a tiny body, a microcosm of all your meridians." Dawn's fingers tapped the inner shell of Angie's earlobe, transmitting an unspoken question. A delicate tracing of the rim of her ear followed.

"I know about acupuncture. Mr. Lam's wife is an acupuncturist, although she was a nurse in China." Angie took a deep breath. Then she added, "A dog was killed at work yesterday."